BUCCANEER

The Early Life and Crimes of Philip Rake

Being a CONFESSION
of the most notorious PYRATE
Philip Rake, from his birth in Bristol
in 1692 to his remarkable crimes in the
Caribbean in 1715.

Also an account of his remarkable
ADVENTURES in Madagascar and his
part in the expedition led by WOODES
ROGERS to the pirate colony of
LIBERTATIA.

Written by a gentleman of Portsmouth

MMXXIII

Buccaneer: The Early Life and Crimes of Philip Rake
By Chris Thorndycroft

2023 by Copyright © Chris Thorndycroft

https://christhorndycroft.wordpress.com/

For Maia for her constant encouragement and my parents for their unwavering support

FOREWORD

In presenting this remarkable manuscript to you in book form, I am completing a journey I began back in 2014 when I was researching my novel *The Rebel and the Runaway: A Tale of Smuggling*. That novel explored the 1748 murders of William Galley and Daniel Chater that occurred in my home village of Rowlands Castle.

As well as the Old Bailey records and the series of pamphlets collected as *The Genuine History Of The Inhuman And Unparalleled Murders* by 'A Gentleman of Chichester', my main source was the private journal of Charles Lennox, the second Duke of Richmond, the man responsible for bringing the smuggling gangs of Sussex to their knees.

Charles Lennox is believed to be none other than the 'Gentleman of Chichester' who penned the *Inhuman and Unparalleled Murders* and his journal provided some fascinating insight into his motivations for breaking up the smuggling gangs, namely his pursuit of a fabulous diamond known as the Molucca Star.

Lennox, and his associates in the Freemasons, were obsessed with recovering this diamond which, through some unknown set of circumstances, had fallen into the hands of a Sussex smuggling gang. The origin of the diamond and its story previous to this was unknown.

Until the spring of 2015.

I received an email from a friend of mine working for the West Sussex Record Office. A document had been found during recent renovations to Goodwood House, the seat of the Dukes of Richmond. Behind some wood panelling in what had once been Charles Lennox's study, a bundle of papers was found dating to the early 18th century. The most remarkable thing about these documents was that one of them mentioned the Molucca Star.

Knowing of my interest in Lennox and his pursuit of the diamond, my friend (who wishes to remain anonymous) was good enough to send me a facsimile of the document. When I opened the file and started reading it, I could barely believe what I had received.

Stuffed behind the panelling of Goodwood House for two and a half centuries was the yellowed confession of a previously unknown pirate by the name of Philip Rake. Put to paper while Rake was imprisoned in Newgate in 1722, the confession is an autobiography of untold value to historians as Rake seemed to have rubbed shoulders with just about every known pirate of that period. Not only that, but Rake is revealed to be a previous owner of the Molucca Star. Charles Lennox, himself a gatherer of documents, had somehow got his hands on this confession which undoubtedly fuelled (and maybe even ignited) his interest in the Molucca Star.

My receipt of the Rake document inspired me to write a chronological precursor to *The Rebel and the Runaway* which was published in 2022 as *Under False Flags: A Tale of Piracy*. Captain Rake appears as a supporting character in this, and I finished that novel feeling that the world deserved to know him a little better. His document (which now resides in the British Museum) has since been published but only in academic circles. There has been much media buzz about it and its importance in our understanding of the Golden Age of Piracy, indicating a strong public interest in Rake's story. With that in mind, I felt it prudent to release the Rake document in book form (albeit in two volumes), with modern punctuation and spelling, as a companion piece to my two novels for the public's enjoyment.

- Chris Thorndycroft, April 2022

PART 1 – BRISTOL, 1692 - 1713

Written in Newgate Prison,
The City of London, England,
The fifteenth day of May,
The year of our Lord, 1722

Sir, please don't think that I'm ignorant of your true intentions. I know you wanted to get to me first before the prison ordinary can sell my story to the mob for sixpence once I am upon the scaffold. I know you and your friend are compiling an account of the pirates of the West Indies, few of which remain to tell their tales in person. You'll be wanting to know of Blackbeard, no doubt. Of Charles Vane, Anne Bonny and Mary Read and all those other characters you and your friend have been scribbling notes on. Aye, I knew them. And I can tell you stories about them that are truer than what you've got from the ale-soaked braggarts in Bristol's taverns. But first you wanted to know about me and how I came to be a pirate. Very well. I'll start at the beginning.

I was born out of wedlock in Bristol in the year 1692, or as far as I can make out. My mother was a hardworking but poor woman. I had three siblings: two older brothers named Paul and Jacob and a younger sister called Celia. We lived in a two-room dwelling on Tower Lane; that long curve of ramshackle houses squashed up against the remains of the old town wall.

My mother used to be a maid in some of the fancy houses in Redcliffe but, through a string of unlucky relationships with men who either died or left her, she fell on hard times and survived by doing seamstress work. It wasn't enough to support five mouths so we all pitched in to help in any ways we could, the nature of which will soon become apparent.

Paul and Jacob's father had died before I was born, and Celia's father was a travelling salesman who didn't stick around to play family. As for my own father, he had always been something of a mystery during my early life. My mother would never talk of him and I only knew that he was still alive because every year, on my birthday, five pounds would arrive by courier.

"This is from your father," my mother would tell me, while my brothers scowled at me in the background. "He might have dismissed me, but he hasn't forgotten you."

My mother remained tight-lipped on the identity of my curious benefactor, despite my best attempts at worming the truth from her. I burned to know who he was, my boyish imagination casting my mother as a secret mistress or perhaps one half of a doomed love affair thwarted by parental ambitions and societal restrictions. As for my father, I pictured him as somebody from lordly or even royal stock; some luminous figure that might one day reach a glowing hand down into those dark, narrow backstreets and lift me up out of them, to set me at my rightful place at his table.

Only once did my mother let anything slip about my father and that was after she'd had too much gin one Christmas.

"They all said he didn't love me," she drawled to herself by the fire. "Well, if he don't love me then why does he send us money, that's what I want to know. Many a man has fathered a bastard and nobody holds them to account for it. Easiest thing in the world for a man. But not your father, Philip. He never forgot us. They made him dismiss me. He didn't want to let me go, I'm sure of it. But they made him. Not proper, of course; a man fathering a child on his maid and keeping both around."

Ah. So he was one of those rich gentlemen with a house in Redcliffe where my mother used to work as a maid. The truth of my conception was suddenly thrust into the sordid light of reality and my romantic fantasies evaporated. There had been no tragic love story, no spurned lover, no forced separation worthy of the novels. My mother was a maid brought low by her master and I was the result of some hurried (and, if I know men, probably drunken) fumblings.

These annual monetary gifts from my father caused a curious blend of joy and prejudice. We ate well for a few weeks and my mother purchased candles and clothing while the pennies lasted. But, while my family would readily help themselves to my birthday money, my brothers would cast sneering looks in my direction. The knowledge that I came from a finer stock was a constant source of irritation for them. They would even call me out on it if I ever ended up in their bad books, as if I could possibly do anything about my own parentage.

"Think you're better than us, eh?" my eldest brother Paul said on more than one occasion. "Well, I don't care who your father is, he still left you in the dirt with the rest of us. He can't care about you all that much."

Five pounds a year aside, life was hard for us and, as I said, we did what we could to help our poor mother. It was my brothers who introduced me to the life of crime that I have struggled to turn from ever since. They were pickpockets and cutpurses. Not real villains given to violence, or at least, nothing beyond the occasional dust up in a tavern. I suppose it was my fault that they got wound up in something more serious. Ironic that the youngest brother should lead his elders astray. They may have been bigger than me, but I was always smarter and braver, such is my curse.

I made my first real ripple in Bristol's criminal underworld at the age of nine or so. This was before my little sister was born and we were in particularly poor straits. Our mother had taken with that wandering salesman that was to be Celia's father. We didn't think much of him and let him know it on several occasions. He returned our feelings with his fists and it was a tense time in our little home on Tower Lane. He was a heavy drinker too and there was always some sort of a flap on.

Every July the St. James Fair is held north of the city. I don't know if you've frequented it or if it has at all changed in the last twenty years but when I was a lad, the fair was the highlight of the year. It was a riotous explosion of noise and colour. People would come from all parts of the country to wage money in the boxing booths or on the bear baiting, watch Punch and Judy shows and imbibe gallons of ale. Fights were common, trollops were out in all their warpaint and I hardly need tell you that the whole thing was rife with opportunities for young thieves.

There is no easier target than a drunk and the fair was always rank with them. We targeted the ones who staggered about alone, waited for them to pass behind a tent or a stall and then either trip them or barrel into them, knocking them on their arses. We'd even help them to their feet, apologising for our clumsiness, before leaving them with empty pockets and not the slightest idea of what had just happened to them.

Drunks might be easy but they rarely had much worth stealing having spent most of their coin on ale. You get wealthy drunks of course, their pockets weighed down with ivory-handled penknives, silver watches and silk kerchiefs. But these marks rarely wandered alone, most having attracted a trollop or two to walk arm in arm with them. And the trollops are the greatest pickpockets of all. While they laid on the charm and the fluttering eyelids, hands would sneak into pockets and rob them blind. My brothers regularly bemoaned having been born boys for nature had denied them the best tools for the job. But once they started taking me along with them, I all but made up the distance.

They had taught me all their tricks, you see. We used to practise on each other in the alley behind our house and they trained me hard and well. By the age of nine I had the fingers of the devil himself and could lift just about anything without being detected. A team of three is a winning number because you can employ the age-old technique of distraction. Two cause a disturbance and, while the mark's head is turned, the third swoops in for the prize. I was small, slim and could work my way around skirts and greatcoats with ease, my little arm snaking in and out of pockets and purses, filching the choicest of scores.

We always took our scores to Sam Spritnel at The Old Bell tavern in the Pithay. Sam Spritnel was a one-eyed villain who ran all sorts of rackets but his main one in those days was fencing stolen goods. Coin was all well and good but we had no way to make any money from the kerchiefs, snuff boxes and other items we pinched and we always wanted to get rid of them fast for to be caught with them on our persons was to be as good as convicted.

Spritnel had connections and could sell on just about anything, after taking his substantial cut of course. We became regular suppliers for him, so much so that he began to think he owned us. We became 'his boys' and he would send us out to rob for him. We never questioned why we were working for a boss, young dolts that we were.

One evening, as the fair grew more raucous with the onset of night, we headed down to the Pithay, our pockets swollen with loot. As we passed along Christmas Street towards our own Tower Lane, we heard footsteps behind us. Turning, I spotted two figures making their way through the gloom towards us.

"Eyes front," said my brother, Jacob.

I wondered what he meant and then realised as two more figures emerged from a side alley up ahead. They stopped in the street as if to block our way. We slowed up, none of us sure what all this was about but sure that it was nothing good. The two other lads behind us had caught up and we were penned in and outnumbered. I recognised none of their faces but my brothers evidently did for Paul said, "William Hacker. What's your business with us?"

"Paul Rake," said the eldest of the boys, apparently Hacker. "Been hard at work, have we? Fair was it?"

"Aye, you should pop along," Paul replied. "There'll still be plenty of rich pickings."

There was a tremor in his voice I had never heard before. He seemed frightened by these boys. My big brother, who regularly knocked me into my place and swaggered about as if he owned Bristol, *frightened* of some other boys. I was disgusted.

"What were your takings?" William Hacker demanded.

"There's plenty to go around," Paul said. "They're just getting started up there. If you head up now, you'll find plenty of open pockets and neglected purses."

"Or I could just take what you've got and save myself the bother," said Hacker with a dirty grin.

"We haven't got much," said Jacob, his voice showing the same fear Paul's did.

"No? Your pockets look a tad full to me," said Hacker. "Empty them out."

"Why should we?" I demanded, the words escaping my lips before the thought of them had even passed through my head.

William Hacker glared at me. "Is this the runt of the family? Haven't seen him out and about with you boys before."

"He's only recently started on the job," said Paul in a quick voice. "He don't mean nothing by it ..."

"Rude little blighter, ain't he?" Hacker pulled an object from his pocket and opened it. I realised it was a clasp knife. "Might have to teach him some manners."

"Look, you're welcome to what we've got," said Paul in that same fast voice as he emptied his pockets. I realised then that he was trying to save me. Would this William Hacker really cut me? Or kill me perhaps?

"Now that's more like it," said Hacker, making the knife vanish back into his pocket as Paul handed over a couple of silk kerchiefs, a fistful of coins, a lady's necklace and, the prize of our efforts, a silver pocket watch.

"What've you got?" Hacker said to Jacob.

Jacob followed Paul's example and turned out a second fistful of coins and four kerchiefs. I watched, appalled as the fruits of our labours vanished into the pockets of strangers. Then, Hacker turned his attention on me. I returned his gaze and kept my hands by my sides.

"Well?" Hacker asked.

"Ain't got nothing," I said, not very convincingly.

Paul cuffed me alongside the ear. "Hand it over to him," he hissed.

The other boys loomed over me. It was clear that they were poised to give me a drubbing or perhaps worse if Hacker's clasp knife was any indication. If it hadn't been for my brothers, I don't know what I would have done. Courage has always been my strong point, although it has got me into some fearful scrapes in my life. I must have been born with it for I don't remember feeling any fear at that moment as I stared up into William Hacker's eyes. Only a burning hatred for these louts who thought they had the right to rob us just because there were more of them than there were of us.

Upon further urging from my brothers, whom I still looked up to at that age, I reached into my pockets and reluctantly pulled out their contents.

"Learn from your brothers, little runt," said Hacker as he pocketed my score. "Or the next time we meet, you might not live to tell of it."

With exuberant chuckles, the four boys drifted away from us and vanished into the gloom. As soon as they had gone, Paul seized me and all but lifted me off my feet, shaking me savagely as he did so.

"Are you mad, you little bastard?" he cursed. "When it's William Hacker and when it's four of them, you bloody well hand over your goods and you be polite about it! You're lucky we had plenty to give him, otherwise he might not have been so soft on us!"

"We worked all day!" I said, feeling a sob of rage choke my words. "And he comes in and pinches the lot without lifting a finger!" I was close to tears with the frustration of it all. It had been my first big score and I was looking forward to bringing my cut home to our mother.

"Well, what of it?" Jacob said. "We had no choice. Hacker is a bastard but he's a mean one."

"Aye, he's already killed a man," said Paul. "You think he'd think twice about a little runt like you? You'd be dead in the gutter without us. Come on, let's get over to The Old Bell and tell Sam what's happened."

Sam, as it turned out, was none too pleased when we came to him with nothing to show for our day at the fair. He was a big man, with an eyepatch over his left eye, covering the result of some ugly altercation in his youth. He was in his twenties and already had a considerable following. A man definitely on his way up in Bristol's underworld.

He often held court in the back room at The Old Bell. Not that he owned the place, but he had strongarmed its owner into paying him protection money and therefore, considered the place his. The owner seemed happy enough with this arrangement for plenty of wealth passed through the hands of Spritnel's gang and Spritnel always made sure his gang paid for their drinks.

The back room was smoky and busy with gang members who sat around drinking gin and beer, plotting schemes and playing cards. Jacob and I followed Paul through the press of bodies to the large oaken table at the rear of the room where Spritnel was found with Catherine Read in his lap. From what I have told you, you will surmise that I knew what a trollop was, even at that age, though I had little idea what one did with them.

Spritnel looked up from Catherine's barely covered breasts and his smile widened as he saw us.

"Aha! My profitable agents return!" he said. "How went your day?"

"Very well," said Paul. "Apart from being robbed by William Hacker and his boys on our way here. They pinched us in Christmas Street and took every last thing from us."

The smile fell from Spritnel's face. "Robbed by that clod?" he snarled. "Two big lads like you?"

"He had three lads with him," piped up Jacob. "We didn't have a chance."

"Where are your bruises, then? Where are your bloodied lips and what's more, your bloodied knuckles? I'll not have it said of me that my boys don't stand up for themselves!"

"We were outnumbered ..." said Paul. "And you can see we had our little brother with us ..."

Spritnel didn't even pay me a glance. "You mean to say that you handed over a day's takings to that whoreson without taking a single lump nor landing a single blow for it?" He was nearly bellowing now and the room had fallen silent. Catherine had wisely made herself scarce and was seeking less volatile customers in the taproom.

"How am I to know that you tell me the truth?" Spritnel went on. "How am I to know that you haven't squirreled the loot away someplace and then concocted this tale for my ears?"

"We haven't!" Jacob squeaked. "Honest!"

"Aye," said Paul. "We wouldn't cheat you, Sam."

"I know you wouldn't, boys," said Spritnel, a dangerous gleam in his single eye. "Because that would be very foolish of you. You know what I do to boys who cheat me?"

My brothers were silent and Spritnel held their terrified gaze for so long that I almost involuntarily said, 'no, we don't. What do you do to them?' I was curious, you see and had no idea at that age of what 'rhetorical' meant.

Neither did Sam Spritnel for he proceeded to explain to us in great detail how he hanged liars and cheats by their thumbs and beat them with a chain until all their ribs were crushed. I could practically feel my brothers trembling on either side of me.

"So then, my brave lads," said Spritnel, pleased to see that his words had had the desired effect. "How are you going to convince me that you really were robbed by Hacker?"

"We'll bring you double the score tomorrow," said Paul. "You'll see. We'll work extra hard to make up for our losses today."

"I'm glad to hear it," said Spritnel. "Because every boy under me has to earn. Those that don't find themselves suffering a similar fate to those who cheat or lie. Is my meaning clear?"

"Aye, Sam," my brothers said with nodding heads.

Apparently dismissed, we scuttled out of there and found a spot to sit in the taproom, not wanting to be under the glare of Sam Spritnel a second longer. I was sent to fetch ale from the pot girl while my brothers quietly discussed how on earth we were going to make good on our promise. We had worked hard that day and the thought of trying to double our score tomorrow seemed like an impossible task.

"What will you do?" asked Mary Read, the pot girl, once I had told her of our predicament.

I considered Mary a friend. She had a snub nose and a light dusting of freckles which gave her an innocent look but boys underestimated her at their peril. I had seen her knock older boys off their feet with a clean right hook on a couple of occasions. She was a couple of years older than me and was Catherine's daughter. Her mother had found her work in the same establishment she plied her own trade in. The Old Bell was quite the source of employment, you understand.

"I dunno," I said truthfully. "Just have to work extra hard tomorrow, I suppose."

"But everybody will be hungover from the fair," said Mary, a concerned look in her eye. "Won't be many pickings on the streets."

Mary had done her own stint as a pickpocket, you see, and had a proper understanding of our trade.

"I could kill that Hacker for pinching our score," I said, filling my voice with the type of bravado boys use in front of girls they want to impress.

She raised her eyebrow at me. "He'd flatten you. Hacker's a brute."

"Hmph," I said, knowing she was right but not wanting to comment any further.

Mary poured us our ales and I took them over to my brothers before returning to the bar to drink mine. I chatted with Mary while she cleaned glasses with a rag. I'd rather talk to her than mope about with Paul and Jacob.

Mary was pretty despite her boyish haircut. She had once told me that her mother kept her hair cut short on purpose. Catherine's husband had been lost at sea some years before and their infant son had died not long after that. That's when Catherine got her bright idea. Her dead husband came from a well-off family in London and she got the notion to scam his mother into financially supporting her. Having fallen into prostitution, Mary had been sired on Catherine by one of her customers and every so often she would take Mary to London dressed as a boy to convince the old bird that her grandson was alive and well. None the wiser, the granddame provided a crown a week for the maintenance of her dead grandson.

That's what life is like in Bristol's backstreets. Everybody has some sort of scam going.

"Well, you'd better think of something," Mary said, not altogether helpfully. "If Sam thinks you've fiddled him, you and your brothers won't be on the streets for much longer. Or anywhere else for that matter."

I ignored her as I desperately tried to think of how we could score enough takings to make Sam happy in less than twenty-four hours. But my mind kept drifting back to William Hacker, my infuriation at being robbed by him not allowing me to forget him. Then it came to

17

me. What better way to refill our pockets than to steal back what had been taken from us?

I hurried back over to my brothers and asked them where William Hacker and his cronies divvied up their takings and which master they paid tribute to.

"They have a spot in an abandoned house down in the harbour," said Paul. "As for masters, how should I know? The harbour gangs are a different breed to us. I don't know what they were doing up on Christmas Street tonight but I imagine they were waiting for easy pickings like us to come back from the fair."

"They'll be celebrating tonight," I said. "Drinking themselves silly."

"What of it?"

"So they'll be out cold tomorrow morning."

My brothers frowned at me. "What are you prattling about?" Paul asked.

I smiled and explained my plan to them. They sneered at first and told me to keep quiet about things I didn't understand. But the more I laid it out for them, the more they came around to the idea. They really began to see that it was possible. Dangerous, yes, but *possible*.

We headed home after that and got some shuteye. The rest of the city revelled in the culmination of the fair but we needed rest as my plan required us to be up as soon as it was light.

With our mother's snores still rumbling from her bunk, we slipped out into the cold blue of the dawn and headed down the street to the old archway that covered the steps leading down into the Pithay. This is all that's left of Blind Gate and the remains of a square tower still stands above the archway; a crumbling ruin that goes by the name of 'Nightingale Tower' these days. The tower, little more than a stone shell, is a regular nesting spot for the gulls that plague the city and their echoing shrieks within its broken walls adds a voice to the legend that the tower is haunted.

We scrambled up the tower as far as we dared and, upon my instructions, began scooping up abandoned nests, crusty with gull shit, and depositing them in a small hemp bag we had brought along for the job. It amused me to see my older brothers scrabbling about in the filth and dodging angry gulls on my orders, but they were confident now that my plan would work. Our bag full to bursting, we clambered back down to Tower Street and then, with the sun rising over the roofs of the city, headed towards the harbour.

Paul directed us to the abandoned house on the other side of the River Frome. It was part of a derelict area near the bridge and the place was deathly silent as we hurried through its shadows. It wasn't hard to find the lair of Hacker and his cronies as the faint plume of a dying hearth fire could be seen drifting from a broken chimney.

The front door was bolted shut and, after circling the building, we ascertained that there was a second story entrance at the top of a flight of stone steps at the rear. Through one of the grimy windowpanes, we could see Hacker and the three others who had accosted us last night slumbering on the floor below. Several bottles were lying around, signs of their celebration at our expense. We climbed to the rooftops and made our way cautiously along to the chimney stack. Jacob tied a long length of rope to our bag of nests and gull shit and we lowered it down the chimney.

Have you ever smelt burning gull shit? It's just about the worst smell there is and it smokes something terrible. As we lowered our little package for Hacker and his boys, it got lodged somewhere in the chimney. Paul and Jacob dropped a couple of roof tiles in after it to try and dislodge it and I hurried back down to the window.

My plan was working for I could see smoke start to billow out from the fireplace and the stink of it through the broken panes told me that our little package had not only blocked the chimney but had also caught fire and was adding its own vile stench to the smoke.

It seemed to take an age for the drunken Hacker and his friends to wake up and notice that something was wrong. The coughing began before they were fully awake and only intensified as they gathered their wits to them. Getting to their feet, they stumbled about, bent over with coughing (Hacker truly living up to his name), cursing and crying out in alarm. In a blind panic, they headed for the door and that was my cue.

Around my neck I wore a kerchief I had soaked in water and this I secured over my nose and mouth. With the house now vacated, I opened the rear door and dashed in.

The smoke was thick and acrid and even with my crudely fashioned mask, I had a hard time of it breathing. A rickety staircase led down to the ground floor which was almost completely enveloped in smoke. My eyes stung as I descended the stairs and I began to regret the whole plan, but there was no turning back now, not now that we were so close.

I began rummaging through the detritus Hacker and his friends had left behind. Bottles, bedding and the rubbish of the house's previous inhabitants formed the bulk of it. It was the loot I was looking for. Surely they hadn't spent it all the night before? It occurred to me that the gang might keep it in a hidden place, and I hoped they didn't for I had no time to tear up floorboards or look for loose bricks in the walls.

There was an old dresser in the corner and I flung open the drawers and rifled them. They were filled with junk: mostly old clothes, newspapers and tools. There was a box, the type a lady might keep her jewellery in, and my heart leapt. I opened it up and there lay most of our loot and then some. Our pocket watch was there along with several guineas worth of coinage and a trove of other items that Hacker's boys had filched in the last week or so. It was an incredible score and I hefted the whole box under my arm only to be more delighted to see a stash of silk kerchiefs padding out the drawer behind it. These I shoved into every pocket I owned until I bulged in all directions, before making my way to the stairs.

Paul and Jacob had to help me scramble back onto the roof and we could barely contain our joy at my haul. On the street below, we could see Hacker and his three companions gazing at the smoke that billowed out of the door to their hideaway, confusion written large on their faces. We kept our heads low for they only had to gaze up at the roof to see the cause of their trouble.

We waited until the sack of nests in the chimney had burned away and the awful black smoke started to dissipate. When Hacker and his boys ventured back inside to investigate, we made our escape, scrambling down from the roof on the other side of the house and slipping away, back towards the bridge.

We took our haul directly to Sam at The Old Bell, triumphant in our victory. My brothers were well pleased with how my plan went off and it was the first time I can remember them looking on me with anything approaching pride.

Sam was still asleep after his own celebrations, so we waited in the tap room and had an early ale to celebrate. Mary was up and attending to her duties and I couldn't resist boasting to her of how I had made good on my promise to make amends with Sam, and at William Hacker's expense too! Her eyes widened at the audacity of my plan and the danger we had put ourselves through and I do believe that she was thoroughly impressed, for once seeing me as more than a nine-year-old braggart desperate for her approval. It had turned out to be a most profitable morning on many fronts!

Sam was happy enough when he finally roused himself and was met with our success. He was hideously hungover of course, but the sight of the box of trinkets and the bundle of silk kerchiefs did its part in blowing away his ill condition. He congratulated us on making good on our promise and we all had a glass of gin to toast ourselves. My brothers said nothing of it being my idea but I suppose I shouldn't have been surprised. Paul, especially, was hardly going to let his nine-year-old brother take the credit for bringing such a score to Sam's door. I said nothing but Sam had thrown me a wink before we drank to our health. That was at least some acknowledgement, and I knew even than that I should be happy enough with it.

And for a while I was.

The tale I have just told you is just one example of the escapades of my youth. I have one more to tell you before we get down to the business of why I had to leave Bristol and, indeed, England, which is where my adventures truly began. The purpose of the following anecdote is to illustrate how far up the ladder I climbed in Sam Spritnel's gang which you might say was the very steps to my damnation and exile from my home country.

I was fifteen in the summer of 1707 and there had been many changes in my life. Fortunately for us, our mother's beau had moved on, spurred no doubt by the news that she was pregnant. Our little sister Celia was born in the winter of 1701 and, despite being another mouth to feed, she was a delight from the very day of her birth. We begrudged her not at all for she was a fine trade for her miserable father.

The other big change that had happened to me was that my father had made another contribution to my life, though not in person, of course. A letter arrived on my fourteenth birthday to inform me that an apprenticeship to Mr. Parker, a cooper near the docks had been arranged for me. I was to be a cooper's apprentice and was to receive an education as well as a promising trade.

You may very well imagine what my brothers thought of this new impudence. If I had been the bastard scion of a nobleman before, now I was to become an educated man and an honest tradesman; something they could never hope to achieve. They may have given me a harder time for it but, in truth, I had earned a little of their respect since the incident with the gull shit. I was a valued member of Sam Spritnel's gang and the brains behind the Tower Lane crew. It was always my plans we acted on and it was largely down to me that we were such good earners.

Naturally, I did not take to my work and new responsibilities. What use did I have for a career making barrels? I already had steady employment in Sam's gang and wanted to be out thieving, not slaving away at hoops and staves for no pay. I took every opportunity to slink off to The Old Bell and re-join my comrades, prompting my master to seek me out and drag me back to the cooperage, cursing me for an ungrateful Tom Idle. Half a dozen times in my first year alone he thrashed me until I could barely stand.

Old Mr. Parker wasn't a bad sort really, and I dare say I provoked and deserved his rage. But life under Sam Spritnel was far more exciting than the drudgery of the cooperage. And there was a damned sight more money to be made under him too, for Sam Spritnel was branching out into smuggling.

Bristol receives gallons of wine and brandy from France but most of the goods landed on its docks come from the transatlantic trade: sugar and rum from Jamaica, tobacco from Bermuda and Virginia and so on. It pours in by the hundredweight and the trick is to get as much of it inland as possible without paying duty on it. It can cost up to a hundred pounds to get the customs officials to turn the other way on a cutter full of contraband, but a smuggling operation can save more than double that in duty. Most of the officers readily take the cash but it was our job to strongarm or blackmail any who had pretensions of honesty.

We were fairly run ragged dashing about Bristol, bribing or intimidating officers, unloading cargo, moving goods about and all of this on top of our usual pinching of valuables for Sam to fence. Nevertheless, I was able to keep my position as apprentice to Mr. Parker. Despite my early resistance to my potential vocation, I gradually learned to buckle down and learn my trade and even became quite skilled at it. Aside from Mr. Parker, none was more surprised by this than I.

Some of my motivation came from the unlikeliest source too. While my brothers sneered at my education and future profession, it was Sam Spritnel who thoroughly encouraged it. He seemed to like the prospect of having an educated fellow with a trade in his gang. Of course, it wasn't long before I discovered his ulterior motives for keeping my nose to the grindstone. A maker of barrels promised ample advantages to a smuggling gang. But all that came later. First I must tell you of how I really earned Sam's attention and ended up saving the whole gang.

Now, the way goods were smuggled back then was that the ship kept two sets of accounts. One showed the true cargo while a second set of books, showing a far lesser cargo, was presented to the customs officers along with the bribe. It was simple really, as long as everybody was on board and no mistakes were made. But the tides and the weather, as many a seaman will tell you, give not a single fart for well-laid plans.

We were summoned to The Old Bell one afternoon and found Sam in an almighty flap. A shipment of rum coming up the Avon had run aground at a muddy little spot called Pill Creek. The ship's crew hadn't a hope of defending the cargo against the wreckers of the notorious nearby village of Crockerne Pill, but Sam was deeply concerned that the ship's false manifest might fall into the wrong hands.

"The *Magpie's* cargo manifest puts me on the spot for trying to smuggle rum into Bristol," he said, frantic at the thought of his burgeoning crime operation being nipped in the bud. "You three," he said to us. "Get yourselves down to Pill Creek and get that manifest! I don't care about the cargo just as long as you get those books!"

Knowing that there would be wreckers picking through the hull, we armed ourselves as best we could with Paul even bringing along a pistol. Usually we didn't have much need of firearms – knives, clubs and a damned good kicking being our usual stock in trade – but we were acutely aware of the fact that we were leaving Bristol. The riverside villages and creeks of the Avon were uncharted territory for us and had their own share of rival smuggling gangs. I was glad that Sam didn't care about the cargo for I was keen to let the inhabitants of Crockerne Pill keep it. All we had to do was salvage a set of books. Simple, no?

Well, getting there was trouble enough. Time was of the essence and, with a six-mile trek downriver, we borrowed some horses. Now, being a city lad, I had never much ridden the foul beasts and, having spent much of my life since then at sea, my experience with them has improved little. Somehow we jolted our way down there and, sure enough, found the *Magpie* heeled over in the muck, her hull splintered open like one of the burst barrels I fixed up at the cooperage. Of the wreckers, we curiously saw none, although there were plenty of others standing around. Some of them were clearly the crew, the cut of their sea cloth and exhausted faces told us that. But there were some other gentlemen in greatcoats, astride horses who seemed to have the situation in hand. On a grassy knoll nearby, lay the cargo of the *Magpie*, already salvaged and drying in the sun.

"Blast it!" Paul cursed. "Riding Officers, or I'm a papist."

"Then we're rumbled!" said Jacob.

"Only if they find that manifest," I said. "Let's see if they have."

I urged my unruly mount down the bank and we approached the cluster of men.

"Were there any casualties?" I called out in the spirit of one set on helping the unfortunate.

"None," replied the leading officer. "The boat hit a mudbank at low tide. It was overloaded and the damned thing nearly cracked in half. Fortunately, we were close at hand to prevent the locals from stealing the cargo. I have sent for carts to convey the whole lot to the customs house."

"The customs house?" I asked. "Are you seizing it?"

"That I am. The ship was apparently carrying two sets of books. A common trick but we have them red-handed in this case. The captain and the tidewaiter have been apprehended for questioning and I shall take the false set of books before Justice Williams. Who are you fellows, anyway?"

We weren't about to implicate ourselves as associates of the *Magpie*'s owner, certainly not now that this jumped-up blunderbuss had got his hands on the manifest. We gave him some cock-and-bull story about 'just passing through' and surreptitiously made our retreat, watched every step of the way by the officers who had grown more than a little suspicious at our appearance on the scene.

"You don't suppose he recognised us?" Paul said as we hurried back to Bristol.

"No," I said. "Why would he?"

"Because I recognised him. That was Bradley Mitchell. I've seen him in the Llandoger Trow. He's a Bristolian."

"Lucky he has a poor head for faces then," I said.

We made for The Old Bell with all haste and gave the bad news to Sam. He blistered the paint on the walls with his oaths but knew that a cool head was needed to get us all out of this mess. At the very least, we had the name of the Riding Officer who threatened our downfall and knew what his plan was. The only things we didn't know were when he intended to deliver the manifest to Justice Williams and what the bloody hell we could do to stop him.

The next day, Sam located the address of Bradley Mitchell on King Street and I feared that he planned to do something rash like threaten him with violence. My brothers and I had strongarmed many a customs official and this Mr. Mitchell struck me as one of the ones who had a head full of noble opinions concerning his duty. A wrong move now might make it all much worse.

But Sam was a cunning bastard and the very next day he informed us that he had Mitchell's maid passing him information at The Old Bell.

"He's heading out tonight," Sam told us around noon of that day. "He's meeting some other Riding Officers at the Llandoger Trow. You can accost him on the Bath Road. I can lend you some guns. I don't care if you kill the lot of them but get me that book!"

Sam was dangerously frantic now and we didn't dare question his plan. But as soon as we had left the back room, we revealed to each other our own terror at the situation we were in. Mitchell could be riding with half a dozen mounted officers. Sam's demand that we accost them like half-arsed highwaymen was suicide. But then, so was failing Sam.

As we drank and contemplated our predicament, I watched Mary pour ale for customers at the bar. She was the regular barmaid of The Old Bell now and popular with the customers. Puberty had given her a fine figure and she wore her hair long now, her grandmother having died some years previously, putting an end to her mother's scam. Mary was no longer the playmate of my youth but a beautiful young woman and, though I admitted it to no one, I was quite smitten with her.

As I watched, a plan began to form in my mind and, without another word to my brothers, I headed over to the bar and explained it to her and the part she would play in it. I was honestly surprised by how vehemently she opposed it. She had never shied away from danger as a child and had willingly got into many a scrape with me. Something about this had struck a nerve.

"Absolutely not!" she said.

"Why not?" I protested.

"Because I'm not a whore!"

"You only need to pick the man's pocket, not fuck him," I said. "And the only way you can get close to him is if you dress up as a trollop. I can hardly do it and he'd recognise me from the other day anyway."

"Listen," she said. "My own mother is a trollop. You think I want to dress up like her, even if it's just to pick a man's pocket?"

"But that's why you're perfect! You can borrow some clobber and some of that grease she paints her face with. She doesn't have to know, and even if she does, I can slip her a few coins to make her happy enough."

Mary shook her head as she cleaned glasses with increased vigour. "She's got worse this year past. Drinks gin like water. Never a sober moment. I suppose it helps her deal with it all."

"My own ma is a demon for the gin too," I said as a weak counterpoint.

"But she's not a whore," she said angrily. "You didn't have to grow up listening to men fuck her in the back room. You didn't see the bruises they left her with. You didn't go hungry because some pimp took most of her earnings for himself. Sam's even started eyeing me up for the trade. I suppose I'm lucky he has waited this long but I won't whore for him. Nor anybody else."

I sighed. Sam had been Catherine's pimp for a few years now and had several other girls working for him too. It was protection of a sort but there was no protecting Catherine Read from herself. She was regularly seen reeling in the gutters having spent every penny she had made on drink. It was little wonder Mary was so averse to following in her mother's footsteps.

"But burn it all, Mary, can't you see what a fix we're in? If we don't get that manifest back for Sam, there'll be hell to pay. And the whole gang might be implicated. You don't want to see me up in the dock facing a magistrate, do you?"

"No but ... surely there is some other way?"

"Oh, aye, there is. Sam wants us to accost them on the road and snatch the manifest from their corpses. He's even giving us guns for the job but my brothers and I aren't too keen on our prospects. Come on, Mary. We can get that manifest before they even set out with no bloodshed!"

She gave a sigh and then nodded. "All right. I'll do it. But God help any man who puts his hand on me."

"I'll be with you every step of the way," I said courageously.

Later that evening, I walked Mary to the hovel on John Street where she and her mother lived. Her mother was still sleeping off the effects of the previous night and I waited while Mary slipped in to get herself ready. When she emerged, my jaw dropped. She wore a dark green mantua drawn back over her hips to expose her contrasting petticoats. She wore no hat but had red ribbons in her hair and the hollows in her cheeks had been brought out by artful brushwork. She regarded me quizzically.

"Don't tell me you like the look of me in this getup."

"Well ..." I stammered. "It's just that I've never seen you look so ..."

"So what?"

I fumbled for words, casting each aside for I knew that she would not be flattered by any of them. But she *was* beautiful, and I felt a pang of jealousy for Mr. Mitchell who was to be the object of her affections that night (even if it was only to rob him).

"Well ... *womanly*," I eventually settled on, wincing a little as soon as I said it.

Mary huffed in exasperation at my clumsiness. "Come on then. Let's get over to the Trow and get this over with. I just hope nobody recognises me."

"I don't think that's likely," I said. "I mean … what with you all dolled up and all."

"Do me a favour and stop talking," she said.

"All right."

"And you should probably loop your arm around mine."

"What? What for?"

"So people will think we're walking together."

"We *are* walking together."

"I know, you dolt, but that way people will think you're my pimp and will leave us alone."

I coloured as much at the thought of being Mary's pimp as I did at the thrill that rippled through my body as she tucked my arm in hers and drew me closer to her. It was strange; a couple of years ago I had felt not the slightest attraction for her in that way. Our bodies had been close before, dozens of times in fact. We had shared hiding spots from bullies and constables and had even fought each other fist to fist on one occasion. But now all had been turned upside down as we walked, arm in arm down Broad Street, her dressed as a trollop and me as a young – and rather unconvincing – pimp. I was aware of the swish of her dress against my thigh and the bulge of her bust so close to my arm. I could smell her hair and realised that she had even put on perfume.

We made it to the Llandoger Trow as it was livening up. I assume you know the place and will know just how large it is, far larger than The Old Bell. We had to move through several rooms jammed with people before we spotted our quarry sitting with two of his associates in a booth tucked away in a corner.

I urged Mary to swing into action while I headed for the taproom next door. She rolled her eyes at me and made her way over, her hips suddenly sashaying the way her mother's did. I knew then that I had been right to put my faith in her. She'd pull it off, no problem.

I ordered an ale and drank it at the bar with my back to the other room. From occasional glances over my shoulder, I could see that Mary had hit it off and was sitting between two of the Riding Officers.

"Oi, is that one yours?" asked the barman, catching me looking into the other room. "I don't allow trollops in here that aren't mine. What makes you think you can graze on somebody else's turf?"

I reached into my pocket and tossed a few coins down on the bar, more than the evening takings of three trollops. "Will that do?" I asked.

"Aye, that'll do for tonight," the barman said, scooping the coins into his apron.

I looked back at Mary and she was doing me proud. The Riding Officers were quite taken with her. Some coarse joke from her lips had them guffawing and one even came up to the bar to fetch more drink. He stood right next to me, and I kept my head down, hoping he wouldn't recognise me.

Before long, the little group in the corner were having a grand old time. Mary was cuddled up to Bradley Mitchell and I forced down my jealousy with the thought of what she was really up to and what was at stake. Her hand was below the table, fondling his thighs. I sucked on my ale and grimaced.

Two more Riding Officers arrived and joined the party. More drink was had and the hour began to grow late. I grew ever more nervous with the waxing of the evening for I had not considered how I was to get Mary out of all this. What if Mitchell wanted to bed her? How far would this game go? I knew Mary would never let him, but I knew also that our cover would be blown if it came to that.

I didn't even know if Mary had the manifest yet but, one by one, the Riding Officers rose (a little unsteadily) from their seats and prepared to leave. One of them, not Mitchell, seemed intent on remaining seated with Mary and he had his arm possessively around her shoulder. Her eyes met mine across the room and I saw a brief flicker of panic cross her otherwise wholly in-character face.

The officer pressed in close for a kiss and I saw our plans unravelling fast. I rose from my seat, not knowing what I could do, only that I must do something. The Riding Officers encouraged the man to get up and join them, but Mary's captor tried to drag her with him. She attempted to wriggle free and her efforts were either unnoticed or ignored by the officer. In the end, it was Mitchell who did my job for me.

"Put her down, Jenkins," he said. "We don't have time to dilly-dally with strumpets."

"Just a quick fumble outside," his subordinate protested. "I'll be quick enough! What do you say about that, my pretty, eh? Tuppence for an upright?"

Mary looked ready to tell the man exactly what she thought of his offer, and I wouldn't have blamed her. I squared my shoulders and readied myself to wade in and fetch her out, not caring how it would look.

"I said put her down!" Mitchell commanded. "We're late as it is and I don't want to keep Justice Williams waiting!"

Jenkins sullenly deposited Mary back in the booth, blew her a kiss and joined his comrades as they trooped outside. I hurried over to her.

"You bloody well owe me for this!" she snapped at me as she finished off a tumbler of gin the Riding Officers had left on the table.

"By Christ, that was a near thing!" I said. "But did you get it?"

She reached inside her dress and pulled out a roll of paper tied with a tatty bit of string. "I don't know if this is what you're looking for," she said, "But it was all he had on him."

I frantically tugged at the string and unrolled the paper. She had done it! It was the manifest for the *Magpie*, showing its falsified itinerary.

"You're a trump, Mary!" I said. "This has saved our necks! Old Sam won't forget this."

"He's not the only one. Now, kindly escort me back home so I can get out of these bloody rags."

I did as she asked and, after leaving Mary at home, I headed back to The Old Bell to hand the manifest over to Sam and to celebrate our success. My brothers met us there, their faces eager for news. I kept them in the lurch and didn't tell them what had happened until I was able to hand the fruits of our labour over to Sam.

To say he was pleased with me was an understatement. I was the toast of the tavern and we all got roaring drunk that night. During the revelry, I caught up with Mary who was collecting glasses and doing her best to ignore her mother as she plied her trade both indoors and out on the street.

"Thank you for helping us out today," I said to her. "I mean it. I'm sorry for what I put your through."

"I swore to myself a long time ago that I'll never end up like my mother," she said, frowning as Catherine Read could be heard whooping at the attentions of some prospective customer in the next room. "I'm going to get out of here, Philip. Out of Bristol. I'm going to make something of myself."

"Like what?"

"I don't know! Just something other than a barmaid or a trollop."

"You won't end up like your mother, I promise," I said, as earnestly as I could manage.

She glanced at me with cynicism in her eye. "And how do you know that for certes?"

"Because I'll marry you and no wife of mine will be a whore."

She laughed at this, and I was a little affronted by her treatment of my sincerity as a big joke.

"I'm serious," I said. "When my apprenticeship is over, I'll be allowed to marry. And I'll make a wife of you on the very day I receive my tools."

"You've got six years ahead of you," she said. "You'll never make it. Not if you keep sneaking back here every time Mr. Parker's back is turned. He'll wash his hands of you before you're twenty-one."

"You'll see," I insisted, surprised by my own sincerity. "I'll make it. And then I'll be a cooper with my own business and plenty of money to keep you in fine dresses. There'll be no more working in this place, you can count on that."

"Very well, Philip," she said. "I'll hold you to that."

"And you'll wait for me?"

She laughed again and this time I didn't mind for it was a seldom and pleasant sight. "Aye," she said. "I'll wait for you."

And now we come to it. The final year of my life in England. 1713. When I would next tread the streets of my homeland, the year would be 1721 and I would be in chains on my way to Newgate.

It was the final year of my apprenticeship. I was twenty-one and aching to be a free man, to set myself up in business and make good on my promise to marry Mary. She no longer worked at The Old Bell, having gone into service to support herself. Her mother had died of the pox two years previously and, keen not to take up the vacancy in Sam Spritnel's stable of trollops, Mary now worked as a maid in one of the fine houses in Redcliffe, just as my mother had once done.

Now, I have previously alluded to the use of my apprenticeship to Sam Spritnel's gang and by the final year of my indenture, I was regularly using Mr. Parker's barrels to cart stolen goods from one end of the city to another. I even stored contraband right there in the cooperage for who would think to inspect a pile of newly repaired barrels? We moved stuff at night mostly and unpacked the goods to be hidden in cellars and haylofts. I would then return the barrels either to Mr. Parker or their rightful owners. It was the perfect scheme.

It was a rainy autumn afternoon that Celia came to visit me at the cooperage which she often did, the reason for which will soon become apparent. My little sister had grown into a lively twelve-year-old, smart as a whip and beloved of us all. Naturally, my brothers and I had taught her the trade of pickpocketing. Money wasn't as tight as it had been in those earlier days for our smuggling operation was booming. But, with us gone most of the time, Celia was alone with our mother whose drinking had not improved. We did our best to make them comfortable but, as far as we were concerned, pickpocketing is an important life skill and besides, our sister had proved to be a good little earner in her own right.

I would pass on whatever she filched to Sam and he would fence it for us. He was impressed with the trinkets she managed to snatch and wanted her to work directly for him. This was something I constantly resisted. I trusted Sam to a certain extent but I'd be damned if I'd let him get his hands on Celia and have her hanging around The Old Bell. She was my sister and I was insistent that I remain the go-between.

It was the for purpose of handing over her latest haul that she visited me that afternoon and I could see that she'd already spent some of her earnings on a lardy cake. She handed the rest over and I admired her industriousness.

"Keep going this way and there won't be a full pocket left in Bristol," I teased.

"Except Sam Spritnel's," she said with a wink. "You going to The Old Bell tonight?"

"What if I am?"

"Toby Rattner's birthday. He's flush at the moment so there'll be a round of drinks for all."

"You're to keep out of that place," I told her sternly. "But tell Toby I might pop by later. I've got these barrels to finish first."

"I thought you were keeping your green face hidden away in here."

"Green face? What are you talking about?"

She grinned with the glee of one who knows something the other doesn't. "You haven't heard, then?"

"Heard what?"

"About your lady friend stepping out with some haberdasher."

"Haberdasher?" Celia enjoyed teasing me about my feelings towards Mary and I assumed this was one of her jokes.

"Honest! Some flashy type with a shop in Surrey is courting her."

"Courting!" I almost bellowed.

Celia paled, realising that her gentle ribbing had awoken a furious passion in me. "I just saw them," she stammered. "Heading into the Elephant Coffee House on All Saints."

I flung down my tools and went to get my coat and tricorne.

"What are you going to do?" she demanded.

"I'm going to see what all this rot is about," I said. "You get yourself home and see to mother. I'll drop by in a couple of days with some coin."

"I'm coming with you!"

"Be off with you!"

The sternness in my voice sent her on her way. I didn't want her with me for in truth, I didn't know what

I would do. It all seemed too far-fetched to have any truth to it. My Mary with some haberdasher from Surrey? Nonsense!

I made my way to All Saints Lane and sure enough, sitting there in the window of the Elephant Coffee House as bold as brass, was Mary Read and some pretentious tradesman with ideas above his station in a blue silk taffeta coat. I flung open the door and stormed into the coffee house.

Mary saw me approaching their table and half rose in alarm, my face evidently showing my displeasure.

"Who's this?" I demanded.

"Philip, this is Alexander Longstreet," said Mary. "Alexander, meet my good friend Philip Rake."

"Ah, young Master Rake," said the silken serpent in a patronising voice. "The cooper's apprentice. I have heard of you."

"Indeed?" I said. "For I have heard not a whisper of you. What do you mean by taking other men's fiancées out for coffee?"

"Fiancée?" said Mr. Longstreet, glancing from me to Mary. "I had no idea ..."

"Oh, Philip is just referring to a foolish notion we had as children," said Mary. "We were sweethearts, it is true, but fiancée is putting it a little strong, wouldn't you say, Philip?"

"The devil I would!" I snapped, causing some heads in the coffee house to turn. "You know as well as I how sincere we were!"

"Philip ..." Mary warned. "We shall discuss this later. At the moment, I am taking coffee with Mr. Longstreet."

"We'll discuss it now," I insisted.

"You heard your ex-sweetheart," said Mr. Longstreet. "She doesn't want a scene and I certainly won't stand for one. Now kindly clear off."

"You'll give me no orders," I snapped at him. "And I'd watch your tone when addressing me."

"Or what?" he replied, fixing me with a dirty glare. "You'll get your gang of ruffians to teach me some manners? Oh, yes, I've heard about them and all your sordid dealings in this city. As if I needed no further incentive to remove Mary from this place and take her somewhere more civilised."

I lost my temper at that and struck him across the face. There was a loud intake of breath from the other customers and Mary snapped my name at me, leaping from her seat to check on her suitor who lay sprawled on the floor.

"You'll regret that, by God!" Mr. Longstreet said as Mary helped him back into his chair. A trickle of blood ran down his cheek from where my fist had split the skin. "I have friends in high places!"

Not caring one jot where he had friends, I turned from the scene and left the coffee house, my head raging and my heart bursting. I was in a dreadful state. Mary and I had never spoken of my promise to her, made all those years ago, but we had remained close companions. Never acting on our feelings for each other, we had been content to remain the friends that we had always been, but secretly I longed for the day I would complete my apprenticeship and wed her. I had always considered her mine, you see, and that afternoon had given me an awful realisation that I might lose her to some other man.

I caught up with Mary at The Old Bell that night, partly to apologise and partly to find out what the hell had been going on.

"I thought I was your man, Mary," I said. "Who's this popinjay you're out and about with?"

"Mr. Longstreet is a very respectable haberdasher," she said. "He has a fine shop in Surrey and has taken an interest in me, that's all. Honestly, the way you two have laid claim to me it's like two dogs over a bone."

"Then you're not going with him to Surrey? You're not going to marry him?"

"I've only met the man twice!"

"Then why are you going out for coffee with him? What interest does he hold for you?"

She sighed. "He's an interesting man who isn't from the back alleys of Bristol."

"What's that supposed to mean?"

"It means he has a future ahead of him. A life somewhere other than here. And that's what I want."

"But I told you I will marry you when I complete my apprenticeship. That's only a year away! Then I'll have my own business and I will take you wherever you wish."

"But you won't, will you? Oh, aye, you'll be a cooper in your own right but you'll be a cooper in Bristol and, what's more, a cooper who is thick with a smuggling gang. You getting your tools from old Mr. Parker won't change anything."

"I can leave the gang if that's what's bothering you ..."

"You won't. You can't. Sam's got his claws into you and he won't let up." Seeing the disagreement in my face, she pressed on; "Besides, would you really give up that life for the meagre wage of a cooper? Face it, Philip. You know as well as I that you can't give it up, even for me. You enjoy it too much. But I have to get out. I'm twenty-three and if I don't want to live out the rest of my days alone and in poverty, then I need to make my plans."

"So you'll just forget me and go off to marry this haberdasher?"

"If he asks me ... I honestly don't know. But I'll never forget you, Philip Rake. That I promise you."

The fight had been knocked out of me by Mary's words. I returned to the cooperage and went to bed, my entire world thrown into upheaval as all the things I had taken for granted were in danger of vanishing like mist in the morning. I felt as if my life was on the precipice of oblivion.

Little did I know how true that was.

It was the following day that the constable arrived at the cooperage and began breaking open barrels. I knew as soon as he showed his thuggish face that I had been peached on and there was little doubt as to who had done it. My rival for Mary's affections was stooping low in his effort to get rid of me. Or perhaps it was his bruised face that drove him to revenge?

The constable found not only contraband that I was keeping for Sam, but various items my brothers and sister had given to me. I was triumphantly escorted to the courthouse where I spent the night until my examination by the alderman in the morning.

They knew who I was and whose operation I was a part of. And they wanted me to tell them everything about it. They wanted names, the quantities of goods we were smuggling, and who the fences for our stolen goods were. I knew nothing I could tell them would be of any use in court if I did not testify and that was something I could never do. It would be my death warrant for a start, but it also went against every fibre of my being to betray men who had been my companions for as long as I remembered.

The alderman raged and threatened. I knew he was after Sam Spritnel and he needed my testimony to use against him. Well, I wasn't moving an inch. He said I would hang for my crimes and the only way to save my neck from being stretched was to cooperate. Wasn't transportation preferable to execution? He could make it happen if I played ball. I told him I didn't care. I wouldn't peach.

I was sent to Newgate after that, not this illustrious place, but Bristol's own Newgate prison on Wine Street, which is a lot smaller and, if it can be believed, dirtier. My brothers joined me there a day later, having been picked up by the constable and found to be in the possession of items recently stolen from a house in Clifton. We knew this was no happenstance. After I had been caught handling stolen goods, it hadn't taken a genius to go after my brothers.

Once I had resigned myself to my fate, I just wanted to get my trial and execution over with. It was all over. Mary was probably on her way to Surrey with her new beau. The bastard had utterly defeated me and Mary was his.

I spent three days at Newgate before I was summoned to a small room where the alderman and two fellows I didn't recognise awaited me. One of them was introduced as Justice Williams; that very same gentleman Mary and I had prevented from examining the manifest of the *Magpie* all those years ago. The other man was a wealthy-looking cove with a powdered wig and face that did not look like it was used to betraying emotion. No introduction was made and he observed us in silence as the alderman and Justice Williams tried once again to get me to testify.

"We have you and your brothers in custody," Justice Williams said, "and can very easily send the three of you to the gallows as 'the Tower Lane Burglars'. The press like names like that and the city can sleep better at night knowing that such a foul group of thieves are no longer among the living. However, we know that you form part of a larger operation that involves smuggling, extortion, bribing of officials and other such thuggery and we are far more interested in hanging those at the top. Give us Sam Spritnel and I can guarantee you and your brothers will face imprisonment instead of the gallows."

"Take a jump in the river."

"This is rather selfish of you," Justice Williams said. "What of your brothers? Their lives are in your hands and you choose to throw them away along with your own?"

"My brothers got me into this game," I said with more resentment than I credited myself with. "They knew the risks before I did."

Justice Williams smiled. "I wish to take a walk. Come with me, Master Rake."

I didn't seem to have a choice. Still manacled, the guard hoisted me to my feet and I was ushered out of the room, wondering what the hell was going on now.

There is a small exercise yard at Newgate known rather cynically as 'the tennis-court' where groups of prisoners are allowed a few hours' exercise at different times of the day. At the moment it was the turn of the female prisoners, of which there were around a dozen, mostly trollops. It was as I spotted a small figure with a tatty cloak wrapped around her moving slowly about between the other wretched creatures that my stomach felt like it had hit the ground. There, cold, scared and hungry, was my little sister Celia.

"Yes, we picked up the youngest member of the Rake clan too," said Justice Williams. "Thievery runs rampant in your bloodline, it seems. Her pockets were filled with items of value that belonged to others. It will be imprisonment for her too, and the value of the items found upon her will result in a severe sentence I'm afraid. It may possibly involve branding with a hot iron."

"She's only twelve ..." I managed.

"Led astray by her elders, I am sure. A tragic tale but not, I fear, an uncommon one."

"You bastard ..." I hissed.

"I could spare her that fate, and her alone. If you cooperate."

"She ... wouldn't be prosecuted?"

"Her crimes are not as serious as those of her brothers. There is little harm in letting a pickpocket walk free when there are far bigger prizes to be had."

As I watched Celia gaze miserably about her, not seeing me, ignored by those around her, I knew I had been broken. My love for her outweighed any sense of loyalty I had for my brothers or the rest of Spritnel's gang.

"If I give you Spritnel," I said. "Do I have your word that my sister will never set foot in the dock?"

"You do."

"And that my brothers will not hang?"

"Merely imprisoned. It is the best I can do for them. They are rapacious housebreakers after all."

"Fine. I'll do it."

I had no choice. We had all taken our chances and Celia, that pure, beautiful light in our lives, was too precious to be caught up in our mess. They wanted Sam Spritnel so I served him up on a platter.

I was held at Newgate for the yearly assizes which were three months away. My brothers were kept in what the prisoners referred to as 'the pit'; a single-windowed hellhole reserved for prisoners awaiting transportation. During that time, other members of the gang I had implicated were rounded up and joined them down there including Sam Spritnel. It must have been the very bowels of Hell in the pit and I felt even more wretched for receiving better treatment. As the lynchpin that held the prosecution's case together, I was kept in a separate cell with access to a dayroom. My fellow prisoners were debtors for the most part, not the thieves and murderers whose company I deserved.

I didn't know how much the others knew of my treachery but they knew soon enough when I faced them in the dock. I avoided their hateful eyes as I read out my testimony that spelled their doom. I can easily play the lion in physical danger and have proven my courage in countless battles since but betraying my family and friends before their very eyes was the worst torture I have ever endured and I wilted before their gazes like a craven.

Indeed, you will notice that I am rushing this portion of my narrative. That is because of all the things I have done, all the misery I have caused in my life, it is these memories of testifying against my comrades that shames me the most. One thing of note throughout the trial was the presence of the mysterious man in the powdered wig who had been at my interrogation. He sat in the public gallery and watched the proceedings with that same fixed stare.

In the end, Spritnel and two others were sentenced to be hanged. Five more, my brothers included, were sentenced to imprisonment, my brothers receiving fourteen years apiece. My sister, as had been promised, walked free and I never saw her again. As for myself, I had expected to join my brothers in prison where I doubted I would survive long considering the hatred I had earned but my own trial never came.

I was taken to that very room in which I had been interrogated and was provided with a bowl of water, a razor and some soap and told to smarten myself up. I had no idea what lay ahead of me now for we had all faced the justice in our filthy clothes and unkempt beards after our months at Newgate. What occasion merited me with a clean shave?

I was taken out of the prison where a carriage waited on the street. Two burly manservants bundled me into it and off we went in a westerly direction. We pulled up at one of the grand newly built houses in Queen's Square and I was quickly hustled in as if the embarrassment of my being seen was to be avoided at all costs.

I found myself in a drawing room with a crackling log fire. A man stood by it, a glass of port in his hand. It was the man in the powdered wig from the trial and I assumed, therefore, that this house was his.

"You have been quite the disappointment to those who invested in you, Philip Rake," the man said, turning to me.

"I wasn't aware of any such investments," I replied.

"Come now, you are not so blindly ungrateful are you? Who do you think paid for your apprenticeship to Mr. Parker? An apprenticeship you have thrown away in your very last year. An utter waste!"

"You ...?"

"I am your father, yes."

I goggled at the man, the man who had been a mystery all my life. The man who had sent me money every birthday, who had apprenticed me to a cooper, but had never shown his face. He was tall, like me, with a narrow face. Powdered wig and fine clothes aside, I could see a little of myself in him and did not doubt for a moment that I now stood face to face with my father. I saw also how I might have looked had fortune favoured me and not left me to fend for myself in the backstreets of Bristol as this man had.

"Tristram Hastings is my name. I am a senior executive in the East India Company and a Tory member of parliament."

"Very impressive," I said, with a slight sneer.

"How much has your mother told you of me?"

"Not a lot. I knew that you were some wealthy cove who once employed her as a maid in Redcliffe but other than that, nothing. Not even your name."

"Perhaps that was wise of her. I loved your mother, but it could never be. One of Bristol's most well-respected merchants taking up with his maid? It was impossible and nobody regretted it more than I."

49

"My mother regretted it more, believe me," I said bitterly. "While you got on with your life of luxury, she drank herself into ruin. Her own children had to thieve to keep her alive. Your measly annual payments did little to help us." If he thought I was going to show him gratitude for his five pounds a year then he was sorely mistaken.

He sighed. "I ought never to have left you in her hands. She was a good woman once upon a time but suffered a weakness of character. But you must understand, Philip, I could hardly have acknowledged you as my own. Imagine the scandal!"

"Yes, *imagine*."

"I did what I thought was best," he said rather abruptly, perhaps sensing my indignation. "And no man may ask more than that. I even provided you with a trade, the waste of which you can hardly blame on me. Do you feel no responsibility for your own actions?"

There were many things I would like to have said to him on that score but I knew it would be futile. A man in his position would never understand the fierce battle for survival on Bristol's streets. I had been raised by pickpockets and had known men like Sam Spritnel since I could walk. Whatever blood was in my veins, I had been born into a violent world of thieves and cutthroats. I did what I did because it seemed the only way to keep my head above the muck.

My father took my silence as a sign of solemn repentance and quickly clambered back onto his high horse. "I have one last favour to do for you, my son. We may not know each other but I couldn't allow you to rot in prison for your crimes, especially after you had turned King's evidence against your comrades. You must leave Bristol for your own safety, and I have arranged the means to do it."

"Leave Bristol?" I said, the concept entirely alien to me.

"I have made arrangements with Justice Williams that you are to be indentured into servitude for a period of seven years. My good friend Woodes Rogers has applied to the East India Company to fund an expedition to Madagascar. The objective is to purchase slaves to be sold in the Dutch East Indies but also to evaluate the suitability of Madagascar as a potential colony. It is a savage and unruly place by all accounts, peopled by primitive tribes and European pirates who have made their homes there. Rogers needs men for his crew and you are to depart on the *Delicia* at the end of the month as an unpaid deckhand."

"You ... you're sending me to Madagascar?" I exclaimed. I had never heard of the place but it sounded like it was on the other side of the world and by my father's explanation, it deserved to be. I began to wish I had been left in Newgate.

My father caught my expression. "You must understand that I do not particularly like the arrangement myself. My own son, bought and sold like a Negro! But it is the only way for you to salvage your life which you have so far squandered. You will become a seaman and learn a valuable trade, not to mention discipline. Once your indenture is over, you may find a career ahead of you. It is the best I can do for you, under the circumstances."

My father made it out that all this was for my own benefit. I didn't believe a word of it, cocky young bastard that I was. All I knew was that my recently revealed father was washing his hands of me once and for all.

My future looked utterly miserable and I honestly wished that I had been taken to the gallows along with Sam Spritnel. To lose everybody I had ever cared for was hard enough, but to be taken out of Bristol, my only home, and dragged across the world to some unbearable hellhole as a slave seemed to me to be the greatest punishment meted out to any of us. Was this my just desserts for betraying my comrades? If it was, then I despised God for it just as I despised my father and myself. I hated all in those days and swore to myself that at the first opportunity I would break free from my bondage and strike out on my own. Such is the arrogance and burning rage of youth! If the world thought to pen me in, then it would have a sore awakening!

PART 2 – MADAGASCAR, AUTUMN 1713 – WINTER 1714

The *Delicia* was a 36-gun merchant vessel outfitted for war. Its commander, Woodes Rogers – my father's friend – was something of a celebrity due to his famous voyage around the world but had been bankrupted by some legal difficulties. Keen to rebuild his fortune, he had used what influence he had to fund a slaving expedition to Madagascar. We set out in late 1713.

Now, I may be a Bristol lad, but I immediately discovered that I had neither the legs nor the stomach for the sea. When I wasn't hurling my guts up over the rail or stumbling about like a drunkard to the infinite mirth of my new shipmates, I was learning the absolute basic operations of the ship at which even the cabin boys and powder monkeys were my master.

At twenty-one years of age, I was far too old to be learning how to tie simple knots or take soundings in shallow water and I found the whole experience humiliating. This was not helped by the other common tars who regularly found opportunity to ridicule me or berate me for a dullard at the slightest misstep.

There is little else I need to relate from our long voyage around the Cape of Good Hope and into the Indian Ocean other than it was the most miserable few months of my life. I missed my family terribly and thought often of Mary, forever lost to me. I eventually mastered my duties but they were toilsome and laborious tasks like standing watch, scrubbing decks and manning the pumps during one of several terrifying storms that assailed us as we followed the coast of West Africa down to its tip. My experience as a cooper's apprentice provided me with some extra employment, however. The ship had its own cooper and I occasionally helped where needed, fixing the water casks which began to leak after a particularly rough storm.

There were the occasional moments of passing interest and even fascination. As we crawled our way up the eastern coast of Africa, we sighted whales; a pod of about a dozen coming up for air and jetting water through their blowholes. Most onboard paid these beasts not a glance but for me they were the first realisation that I had entered a wholly different part of the world and one I had never thought to venture into.

We reached Madagascar in March 1714 and put in for water and supplies at Port Dauphin, a trading post on its south-eastern tip. The settlement was run by a retired pirate by the name of Thomas Collins who had made his fortune plundering Moorish shipping in the Indian Ocean before he decided to take over the French East India Company's failed colony.

Such a degenerate warren of filth and debauchery I had never seen. The brothels and taverns of Bristol's waterfront paled in comparison to this den of the worst scum who had fled from Europe for these warmer climes. The old fort was still in existence, though it was a ruin of a thing only partially occupied by Collins's gun batteries. The rest of the town was a collection of tents, shanties and huts in the native style. It was my first experience of a pirate settlement and it was far from my last.

We saw no other ships there and there seemed to be a sense of desperation about the place. Rogers went ashore to discuss the purchase of slaves with Thomas Collins but he returned by evening, his negotiations apparently bearing no fruit. Now, the way slavery works in that part of the world is that a man in charge, like Collins, acts as the middleman between visiting traders and the native chiefs further inland. He charges a hundred pounds for a ship to do any business in his port and the natives would sell Collins slaves, either from their own stock or they would hunt some down from an enemy tribe, in exchange for powder, shot and other things they had a use for.

The next day we sailed up the east coast of Madagascar and made for Saint Mary's Island, a long, slim island off the Madagascan coast. This too was lorded over by an ex-pirate, a Dutchman by the name of John Pro.

Here we did find another ship at anchor, a 190ft brig called the *Azrael*. It was clearly a pirate ship and in a poor state at that. It had few guns and looked like it needed careening badly, not that I knew much about such things back then. Its crew were wary of us, and well they might be of an East Indiaman, the company being their usual prey in those waters. But Rogers wasn't interested in pirates and, as at Port Dauphin, he went ashore to speak with the self-made governor while the crew busied itself taking on supplies and trading with the natives.

We were given shore leave and most of us headed to the nearest tavern where we encountered the crew of the *Azrael*. Most of us wanted nothing to do with pirates and steered clear but a few of the older hands, those who had perhaps sailed in such company before signing on with Woodes Rogers, struck up acquaintances with the rogues and spent a good evening drinking with them.

I found myself sharing the anchor watch with these same men the following night. An old salt by the name of Walters was chief among them. Then there was Harrison and Rogers (no relation to our illustrious commander) and a Jew called Solomon. They were a tight-knit group whom I gathered had sailed together in earlier days. I never had much to do with them and they kept to themselves, never paying me much notice for which I was glad. As I went below, I overheard them talking, partially screened by a bulkhead.

"I tell you, Walters," said Solomon, "That old brig is the best chance we are likely to see. We always knew that there are too few of us to crew the *Delicia*. If we don't make our move now, then we risk being stuck on our present course which, it need not be made plainer, is the wrong one."

"But will the crew of the *Azrael* be convinced?" asked Harrison.

"Aye, and we'll have to go shares with them," added Rogers. "There's at least eighty of them. That's less profit for us."

"You always knew we'd have to go shares with somebody," said Walters in a gruff tone. "Whether it's the crew of that old tub or this frigate, what difference does it make? Besides, there's enough loot at Libertatia to go around. Let's not get greedy, for greed has been the ruin of many a good plan."

The word 'Libertatia' made the hairs on the back of my neck stand on end and, if I had been cautious not to be seen overhearing before, then I was doubly so now. Libertatia was a myth, a fable written large in the tales of old sailors in the taverns of Bristol or printed in romances. It was the name of a pirate colony in this part of the world founded by the legendary buccaneer Henry Avery as a free republic, safe from the European powers. Many said that it didn't exist and was just part of Avery's legend; a mythology that also told of how he had robbed the Grand Mughal's fleet on its way back from Mecca, abducting the Mughal's daughter and taking her away to his hidden pirate kingdom to be his wife.

"And, speaking of good plans," said Solomon. "How far have you come in winning some of this ship's hands around to our side?"

Walters grumbled. "One or two perhaps. But none I'd trust completely. There's plenty of unsatisfied souls aboard but the tricky part is getting them to believe strong enough to risk it. Many think the stories of Avery's kingdom are no more than wild fancy."

"Even if they know that we were Avery's men who helped him build Libertatia?" asked Harrison. "That it was us who spilt our blood across the Indian Ocean in the gathering of his famous treasure, and that we are the only ones who know where it's hidden?"

"More tall tales," said Walters. "What sailor hasn't met someone who claimed to be associated with Henry Avery?"

"Well, there it is, then," said Solomon. "Our only option is to jump ship and convince the crew of the *Azrael* to join us."

"Aye, but when is it to be done?" asked Harrison.

Any further discussion was cut short by the sound of eight bells signalling the end of the watch. The men dispersed and went to their duties and I hid myself in the shadows as they passed by, not so keen for them to learn that I had overheard all.

It was clear to me that Walters and the others had once been pirates under the command of the legendary Henry Avery and that Libertatia was no myth but a real place somewhere in those waters. Avery was often called 'King of the Pirates' before he had vanished without a trace. That nobody knew what had happened to him made him as legendary as his pirate utopia. Now, that I had learned that Walters and his men not only knew where Libertatia was but knew that Avery's treasure was hidden there, it was almost too much for my mind to cope with. Here I was, a miserable indentured man with nothing ahead of me but years before the mast and no prospects other than slowly working my way up to a position of respect while some of my shipmates were talking about jumping ship and sailing off to some hidden kingdom filled with riches.

To say that I wanted to join them was an understatement. I would have cast all to the wind and thrown my lot in with them in a heartbeat if the opportunity had presented itself. But there was the rub; how was it to be done? I may have hated my current situation but I was no mutineer. The punishment for mutiny was the noose or at the very least a fierce flogging. One man had been flogged on the voyage east for pulling his knife on a messmate and it had been a gut-churning experience for us all. If I was to risk my own back or my very neck, I would need to be certain of the plan's success.

I was driven to distraction the following day trying to puzzle it all out. I agreed with Solomon that our best chance was to jump ship. From what I knew of our other shipmates, they were dull fellows lacking the courage and sense of adventure required for the task. Besides, there wasn't one of them I trusted nearly enough to bring in on the plan. And come to think of it, why would Walters and the others trust me?

Whatever decision I might have come to that day was rendered obsolete for, the next evening, Walters, Harrison, and Rogers were seized on orders of the first mate and clapped in irons. Solomon was nowhere in sight and, as Walters and his co-conspirators were dragged below, I was in no doubt that he had already been captured and had peached on the others. I thanked God there and then that I had not thrown my lot in with them for I too would be joining them in irons.

It was clear to the captain and Commander Rogers that some conspiracy had been unmasked and, despite not knowing quite what it was, they were keen to root out any fellow conspirators. One by one, every member of the crew was summoned to the Great Cabin to be interrogated by the captain.

As we waited in the forecastle for our names to be called, we could hear the screams of some wretch below. Commander Rogers and the first mate had accompanied the prisoners into the gunroom and it seemed apparent that they were using brutal methods to winkle more information out of them. We sat pale-faced in the moonlight thanking our stars it was them and not us, but I couldn't shake the uneasy feeling that such savagery meant that Rogers was after more than the names of fellow mutineers.

When I was called up, I was interrogated at length by the captain regarding my relationship with the prisoners, how well I knew them and if I had heard of their plan to mutiny. Solomon, it turned out, had been seen meeting with the crew of the *Azrael* and had been overheard mentioning jumping ship. Captain Gregory wanted to know if I knew anything of this or if I had been asked to aid them in any way. I did my damnedest to persuade them that I knew nothing.

As we were just finishing up, Commander Rogers entered the cabin. The sweat stood out on his brow and he looked to have been exerting himself somewhat. He glanced at me and frowned. It was the closest I had ever been to our commander and the nearby lamp illuminated the horrific scarring on the left side of his face courtesy of a Spanish musket ball that had shattered his jaw earlier in his career. In that same battle he had also been wounded in the leg by a wooden splinter, giving him a limp for life. My father's friend, despite his well-known financial problems, was quite a formidable figure.

"Who is this man?" Rogers asked, casting a curious glance over me.

"Philip Rake," said Captain Gregory. "An indentured man with little to no experience. He knows nothing of the mutiny in any case."

"Ah *yes* ..." Rogers muttered. "The bastard spawn of my good friend Hastings. What is it they say about the apple falling far from the tree? A great distance in your case, Rake."

I said nothing, although I dare say my face said a good deal.

"Have you broken the prisoners?" Captain Gregory said to Rogers, my presence in the cabin forgotten for the time being.

"Not yet," Rogers replied. "While the others have admitted to being Avery's old crew, the one called Solomon apparently never sailed with them and nothing

I did to him could make him reveal anything of use. The others remain tight-lipped, but I will pursue my interrogation of them tomorrow."

"Did they know of our mission before they wormed their way into my crew?"

"I dare say they did for it would be too much of a coincidence otherwise. We did our best to keep tongues from wagging but wag they did and some of Avery's old crew must have jumped at the chance. Fortunately, we were able to stop them from fulfilling their plans. Now, I am tired, and it will do the prisoners good to stew overnight. I'm for my cabin. Wake me if you find anything out from the crew though I suspect they'll be just as clueless as my friend's son here. If any others were in on the plot, then Solomon would have surely named them by now."

I shuddered to think what Rogers had done to Solomon but the knowledge that there had been some clandestine aspect of our voyage roused my curiosity. I glanced at the papers on the captain's table. It was an untidy mess and atop a pile of documents was a pamphlet, the type that is sold for a shilling on Broad Street back in Bristol. A name on the cover caught my eye. *Avery.* It seemed to be a lurid 'life and crimes' type of piece by somebody with a Dutch name.

I realised then that Rogers was looking for Avery's lost kingdom and that this whole voyage with its pretence of buying slaves was really a treasure-hunting expedition. It only increased my confidence in Walters and the others. If Rogers was also looking for Libertatia then it had to exist!

I was dismissed and made my way back up to the forecastle, my head buzzing. It was agony to be so close to the call of freedom and riches and be unable to answer it. I found myself angry at the men imprisoned below for bungling their own plan. They might be aboard the *Azrael* that very night, sailing for their lost kingdom and I with them! Now they were under guard, denied their chance to reclaim their fortune.

The more I thought about it the more I realised that it was but a few of our own shipmates that stood in the way. Rogers had retired to his quarters, the captain was in his cabin and most of the crew were ashore. I doubted if anything more than a single guard watched over them below and as for the watch on deck, that would be only two men, one of whom would be me that night.

A plan began to form in my head and the more I thought about it, the more promising it seemed. After four bells, I took my position on deck with a young sailor called Toby Mulligan and I knew that this would be my only chance. After taking a turn on deck, I slipped below and scouted the state of things. I had been right about a single man guarding the prisoners. It was one of the older sailors, a trusted hound of the captain and I knew he would take some convincing.

I went back up to Toby and told him to help me lower the longboat. He was an impressionable lad and keen to do his duty, so I span him some cock and bull story about Commander Rogers wishing to go ashore and ordering me to prepare the boat. Toby regarded me suspiciously but complied. Once the boat was bobbing in the water alongside the ladder, I told Toby to hold the line while I went and informed the commander that it was ready.

I went back to the gunroom and drew my knife. Before the guard knew what was happening, I was upon him, my free hand grasping for the pistol in his belt which, had he a chance to draw, would have brought my little mutiny to a sudden and bloody halt.

He glared at me with a mixture of outrage and terror as I pointed both of my weapons at him.

"Open the door," I told him.

"You'll hang for this, by God!" he snapped.

"Only if I am forced to kill you," I replied with a grim smile. "Quickly now!"

He turned and opened the door to the gunroom. Once it was open, I struck him on the head with the butt of my pistol. He tumbled headlong and lay still on the floor. I shoved him inside the gunroom and closed the door after us.

The gunroom was dingy. No lamp burned and the only light came from the small window at the rear of the room. I could make out the shapes of the prisoners lying on the floor. They gazed up at me with incredulous eyes.

"Who the devil ..." said the husky voice of Walters. "Is that you, Rake?"

"Aye," I said. "Are you bound?"

"Hand and foot. With rope."

I knelt down and began to cut through the rope that bound Walters' feet together. "We don't have much time," I said as I handed him the knife. "Free the others."

"What's going on, Rake?" asked Rogers. "Why are you freeing us?"

"Because I want to join you. I overheard you talking the other night, about Avery and Libertatia. But don't worry, I wouldn't peach on you. I want a way off this ship and I want some of that treasure you boys are after. Now, if I get us all out of here, will you cut me in?"

"Lad, you've got balls of steel, I'll say that," said Walters. "And if we ever get to our destination, we'll make a rich man of you. But have you a plan beyond braining the guard and cutting our bonds?"

"Aye, Toby is waiting with the longboat lowered. We can cut across the harbour to the *Azrael*."

"Toby Mulligan?" Harrison said. "Is he planning on joining us too?"

"Not that he's aware of," I said. "Where's Solomon?"

"Over there," said Walters. "That bastard commander put hot iron to his flesh. He's barely conscious."

I crept to the rear of the small room and nearly tripped over the prostrate form of Solomon. He groaned and by the moonlight I could see the nasty patches of seared flesh on his naked chest.

"He gave us up but he couldn't tell them anything about where Libertatia is for he's never been there," said Walters.

"It was to be your turn tomorrow," I said. "Rogers wanted to let you stew first."

"You're a godsend for saving us from that fate," said Harrison. "And I for one will gladly see you get your share."

"Let's get off this tub first," said Walters. "Lead us out, Rake."

Stepping over the unconscious form of the guard, we headed back up the companionway to where Toby was awaiting my return and expecting to see Commander Rogers with me. When he spotted the four prisoners – Solomon supported by Harrison and Rogers – I feared that he would raise the alarm. His face paled as I quickly brought my newly acquired pistol to bear on him. I told him to standby as we got Solomon down the ladder.

"What's going on?" he said with a quiver in his voice as the prisoners clambered over the side.

"We're jumping ship," I replied. "And you're coming with us."

"Not I! I'm no deserter!"

I jammed my pistol into his chest. "You'll do as you're told and if you're a good lad, we'll put you off someplace where the crew of this damned tub can pick you up. Now get down into the boat."

I held the line while Toby, damn near sobbing with terror, descended the ladder. Then, letting the line slip and shoving my knife and pistol into my belt, I hurried after him.

We shoved off and cut across the water towards the *Azrael*. Walters hailed them in as loud a voice as he dared and, upon recognising my companions, the anchor watch gave us permission to come alongside and board.

I let Walters do the talking and thought it a lucky thing that most of the men on anchor watch had been the ones from the tavern the previous night. The captain was also aboard – a rotund man with a purple silk sash around his paunch – and he came swaggering out of his cabin demanding to know who had been allowed to board his ship.

"These are the men from the tavern the other night," the *Azrael's* first mate explained.

"Avery's men?" the captain said. "The men who claim to know where Libertatia is?"

"That's us and if you want a share in Avery's treasure, then now is the time to weigh anchor and claim it!" said Walters.

"Not so fast," the captain replied. "How can you prove to me that you speak the truth?"

"Why else would we desert our ship and seek passage on yours?" I put in. "We have run a great risk tonight."

"What's wrong with your companion?" the captain asked, eyeing Solomon.

"He was tortured," I said. "Our plan to join with you was discovered and we barely made it off the ship with our skins."

A cry of alarm carried across the water. We all glanced in the direction of the *Delicia* and saw several heads running fore and aft. Our escape had been noticed.

"We don't have much time!" I said. "You must weigh anchor now before the *Delicia* can block our escape!"

"Why would this Commander Rogers of yours spend such effort to recapture a handful of deserters?" the captain asked.

"Because he also seeks Avery's kingdom and has learned that my companions know where it lies. He will stop at nothing to recapture us and torture its location out of us. We must leave now!"

"But half my crew are ashore!"

"We are more than enough to steer the ship to its destination," said Walters. "Let us lead you to untold riches!"

"Besides," I said. "With only half a crew, you'll all have a bigger share."

The crew of the *Azrael* glanced at one another and even the captain seemed to be coming around to the idea. "Very well," he said. "If it must be now then that's all there is to it. We'll just have to pick up more hands on the return voyage."

As he began giving the orders to depart, I thought myself lucky not a member of his crew to be so easily discarded. But we were aboard and, if we moved quickly, there was nothing Woodes Rogers could do to stop us.

We let the terrified Toby Mulligan row back to the *Delicia* in the longboat and, with our sails unfurled and luffing in the warm night air, we got the *Azrael* underway. The men aboard the *Delicia* could see that the *Azrael* was making a hasty departure and no doubt suspicions of our being aboard were being voiced. There was no time to weigh anchor so the cable was cut and we began to make our progress out of the bay.

More cries of alarm sounded aboard the *Delicia* and we could see men running up and down the ratlines in an effort to get her underway. She hadn't a hope of catching up to us for we had already come about and had our bow pointed in the direction of the bay's entrance. My only concern was that Rogers would give the order to sink us rather than let us slip away.

Just as I feared, puffs of smoke appeared beneath the window of the Great Cabin as its stern chasers fired their shot at us. Hot metal sailed across our larboard bow, missing us by less than a yard. There was no attempt to fire back; all hands were needed to ensure our escape and the only objective was to put as much distance between us and the *Delicia* as possible.

As we drifted out of cannon range we gave up a loud cheer. The *Delicia* was still struggling to get underway and we were out of the bay and on our way. We were free! I have never felt such exhilaration as I did in that moment as the sails of the *Delicia* dropped away behind us! After months of misery where I had been little more than a slave, I had finally broken away and was in charge of my own future. The knowledge that I was now as good as a pirate lurked in the back of my mind like a grim thundercloud, but I did my best to ignore it.

Walters immediately went below with the captain, whose name we learnt was Tomkinson, to plot our course. Libertatia, I can freely tell you now, lies in a sheltered bay on the north-western coast of Madagascar. As we rounded the northern tip of the island, we were hit by high swells and strong winds. All the progress I had made in banishing my seasickness went over the proverbial side as we were tossed and hurled about with terrifying force. Mercifully, the winds dropped once we had rounded the tip and began making our way south along the coast. Everybody complained about the lightness of the wind which constantly shifted direction and made our going very slow but personally I was glad of the reprieve.

I spent much of our voyage in discussion with Walters on his adventures with Avery and the truth about the fabled pirate republic.

"I saw a pamphlet on the captain's table aboard the *Delicia*," I said. "Avery's life and adventures written by some Dutchman."

"Adrian van Broeck," said Walters with a nod. "The man's a liar. We took him on as a crewmember after we had left the East Indies for the Caribbean. He scribbled that rag as soon as he got back to England and made a small fortune telling lies about Avery. Had him marrying the Grand Mughal's daughter after we plundered his fleet which was utter nonsense. There was no Indian princess aboard those ships. And Avery was no rakish womaniser."

I detected a hint of malice in Walters' words that spoke of bitter memories. "You were part of the raid on the Mughal's fleet?" I asked.

He nodded. "Aye, myself and many others. We joined with five other captains in the straits of Bab-el-Mandeb in August of 1695. Avery was elected commodore and we lay in wait for the convoy of twenty-five Mughal ships on their way to Surat. Due to a starless night and a drunken lookout, they slipped past us in the night and we had to give chase. It took us a couple of weeks to catch up to them. We went after the *Fateh Muhammed* first and she put up a deal of resistance but we captured her. Two days later we came upon The *Ganj-i-Sawai* which was the cream of the crop, belonging to the Mughal himself. It boasted eighty guns but we were able to cripple her and they soon struck their colours. We boarded her and what followed was several days of slaughter and savagery."

Walters' eyes had a distant look in them, as if he was seeing past the red hills of Madagascar to an uncomfortable chapter in his life.

"Once aboard, the men lost control," he went on. "There was no daughter of the Mughal aboard but there were plenty of other women and what they were subjected to would burn the hardest of hearts. As for the men, they were barbarously used. It is to my eternal shame that I was ever a part of the whole thing."

"So van Broeck was never at Libertatia?" I asked.

Walters scoffed. "Van Broeck couldn't even get Avery's name right. He called him 'John' in his pamphlet when anybody who knew Avery knew his first name was Henry. And van Broeck certainly didn't know where Libertatia was for we never told him. That's why he put in some rot about it being on St. Mary's."

"And that's why Rogers made for St. Mary's," I said. "The voyage was never about buying slaves. He was looking for Libertatia."

"And if all he has to go on is van Broeck's load of nonsense, then he'll never find it."

"But we will?"

Walters smiled. "We know where it lies; Harrison, Rogers and I that is. For we were the ones who built it with our own hands!"

"Is there much treasure there?"

Walters scratched his greying side whiskers and tried to conceal his mirth. "Oh, more than enough to satisfy you, young Master Rake. Though how many of our old shipmates are left there to share it with I have no idea."

"Shipmates? You mean there are still some of Avery's crew in Libertatia?"

"Aye. Little more than maroons, poor buggers. You see, after we had robbed the Grand Mughal's fleet, we were hunted men. The East India Company put prices on our heads and we had just about every privateer in the Indian Ocean playing pirate hunter. Although were filthy rich, we had to lay low for the time being. Food began to run scarce and it became clear to us that we wouldn't survive much longer. There began to be talk of sending the *Fancy* – Avery's ship, that was – with a crew to Malabar to purchase rice and other supplies out of the common account. It was then that Avery made his plan known to me and several others of his most trusted companions. He wanted to leave Madagascar with as much of his treasure as he could carry. Things were getting too hot in the Indian Ocean and he had a mind to sail to the West Indies where we would be less hunted. But there was just too much loot and too many men to carry with us. That's when we decided to betray our comrades."

"Betray?" I asked, astounded.

Walters nodded, his eyes staring at the coastline as it drifted past. "The *Fancy* was fitted out and sent on its mission. I was part of its crew but we had a hidden agenda. We sailed north and waited in a secluded cove while Avery and a chosen few loaded as much treasure as they could onto an ox team and slipped away under the cover of night. They only took what might easily be divided among us – diamonds and small chests of pieces of eight – leaving the larger and more costly treasures behind. We met up with them at the cove, secured the treasure onboard and then departed for the West Indies."

"Marooning your comrades on Madagascar," I finished for him.

"Aye."

I began to realise that ditching half your crew was common practice for pirates.

"It was always Avery's intention to return for there was one treasure we had left behind that was more precious to him than all the rest. The Molucca Star."

"The Molucca Star?"

"A very large diamond. As big as a bullock's eye. We took it from an East Indiaman bound for England. It was far too valuable to take with us for there was no way of selling it without attracting attention. It tore Avery's very heart from his breast to leave it behind for I believed he loved that diamond more than anything he had ever loved. But fate has a cruel sense of humour."

"He never returned?" I asked, remembering how the eventual fate of Henry Avery was a mystery.

"We ran into bother in the Caribbean and had to make our way back to England. We spent or lost most of our wealth and Avery was conned out of his diamonds by some likely types in a Bristol tavern. He spent the rest of his life trying to scrounge together the means to fit out a ship and return to Libertatia but died before he was able to."

Walters sniffed the sea breeze and gazed at the red hills that slipped by. "I'm an old man, Rake, but I may have years in me yet to claim that which Avery could not and die a rich man."

I felt the dull thud of my heart as I thought of the Molucca Star waiting for us in Libertatia and a fear gripped me when I considered the possibility that it was no longer there. "Is there a chance that the maroons found passage off Madagascar since you left?" I asked him.

He shrugged. "It was always a possibility."

I gritted my teeth. "A fine thing that will be if we turn up and find only ruins and the treasure gone!" I kept my voice low, so our new comrades would not overhear. "How do you think Captain Tomkinson and his men will react if that's the case!"

"This life is full of risks, lad," he told me. "But I doubt your fears will be realised. Northern Madagascar is rarely visited. That's why we chose it for our kingdom. Twenty years might pass before a ship thinks to put in at that remote bay. My only fears are what state we might find our old comrades in and what sort of a reception they might give us."

His words filled me with a new sense of trepidation. It had been twenty years since Avery had deserted those men. How wild might they have become in that time and was it long enough for them to forget old grudges?

The bay we were headed for was called the Bay of Narinda and as we entered it, we passed several magnificent mushroom-shaped islands topped with greenery that seemed to blossom out of the turquoise water. White beaches crusted a line of deep-green palms and reddish hills rose behind them that swept away into dusty plains. A river emptied into the bay and we could see from the taffrail that its mouth was guarded by two forts on opposing sides. A double palisade of sharpened timbers surrounded each as well as a ditch. Watch towers and gun platforms could be seen but we could detect no activity in either fort. No colours flew and no smoke from cookfires drifted in the perfect blue sky. The place looked deserted. Captain Tomkinson ran up signals in an attempt to draw the attention of the inhabitants.

"No guards," said Rogers. "I don't like this."

Walters said nothing but I could see his knuckles glowing white as he gripped the rail.

A longboat was prepared and myself, Avery's men and the captain along with some of his crew got into it and we rowed to the northern shore of the river. We beached the craft and, weapons drawn, made our way up the slope to the fort's entrance.

The palisades were ramshackle affairs made primarily of local timber but I could also see the spars of cannibalised ships woven into the architecture. The gate was a large thing that hung a little slack on its hinges of rope and, after our knocking and hallooing drew no response, we cut one of the doors down and entered the fort.

The place was deserted but there had been no sign of a battle. Several huts had fallen in on themselves, their thatched roofs black and mouldering. There were still guns on the platforms indicating that however the inhabitants had left, they had not taken much with them. The sea breeze blew through the deserted place like the whispers of ghosts.

"There's nothing here!" Captain Tomkinson raged, turning a resentful face on Walters and myself. "No pirates, no treasure! Avery's kingdom is a forgotten ruin!"

"I suppose they found passage off Madagascar," said Rogers. "Blast them!"

"*Somebody's* here," I said.

I was the first to see them, emerging like phantoms from the ground as it sloped down north of the fort. Everybody followed my gaze and immediately drew their weapons.

The newcomers wore little clothing apart from the Madagascan *lamba* which is a rectangle of cloth wrapped around the body. Their black hair was worn in a variety of styles and each of them was adorned with necklaces of beads and wristlets of copper and gold. They carried small round shields covered in cow hide and all had spears apart from their leader who pointed an antiquated musket in our direction.

"Malagasy natives!" Captain Tomkinson growled.

"I'm not so sure," said Walters. "Their skin is lighter than any Malagasy I've ever seen."

He was right. While the Malagasy are not as dark as the negroes of West Africa, these men had the creamy complexions of mulattoes.

"English?" said the leader with the musket.

"Yes ..." Walters replied. "English. You speak English?"

"Yes," came the reply. "You come with us."

"Why?"

This caused a stir of irritation and spears were jabbed at us threateningly. We might have fought our way out of there but not without great cost to our number. Besides, I suppose that the others thought, as I did, that by following these people to their chief we might learn what had happened to the pirate colony.

We were allowed to keep our weapons and were treated with a degree of respect along with some trepidation as we were led out of the fort's northern gate and down the slope to a red plain dotted with scrubby bushes and stunted trees. They took us to their village which was not a great distance from the fort and situated in the middle of a dense wood of thorny trees. An embankment had been built around the settlement in the manner of a labyrinth with the intent to confound enemies through which we were led single file taking many turns before arriving within the enclosure.

The village consisted of scores of thatched dwellings made from rough-hewn planks along with several storage huts and kitchens. There were also some tents made from very tattered and patched sailcloth. We attracted a great deal of attention. People crowded around us, staring and talking to each other excitedly. Most had the same creamy-brown complexions of our captors while some were darker like the Malagasy we were used to seeing. I even spotted a few elderly men who could not have been anything other than white Europeans gone native. There were children too, running between the huts in little clusters, pointing excitedly at us. All wore the wrap-around lembas made from cotton or the fibrous inner bark of a certain type of tree as well as the adornments of bead, bronze, copper and gold.

The chief's house was the largest and occupied the centre of the village. It was palatial compared to the huts that surrounded it and was built in a wholly different style. Square-cut beams of large timbers formed a blockhouse with square windows on all sides. The roof was thatched and a hole in the centre emitted thin wisps of smoke. We were led to its entrance and then disarmed. There was nothing we could do about it now for we were in the lion's den and any resistance would end in certain death.

The interior of the blockhouse was dim and smoky and, as our eyes grew accustomed to the darkness, I could see that, apart from its construction, there were several other things about the house that identified a European hand in its construction. A stone fireplace occupied one wall and a chandelier hung from the ceiling. A long mahogany table stretched the length of the room with several silk-upholstered chairs on either side. There were other, more exotic touches such as the Persian carpets that covered most of the flagged floor and the rich, oriental tapestries that hung from the rough-cut log walls.

A white man lolled on a dais of silk cushions at the head of the hall. He was at least fifty, his tangled grey hair long and matted. He was naked but for a lemba and wore a gold disc on his forehead which, as far as I had gathered, indicated nobility among the Malagasy. Two women sat with him, pouring him drink and feeding him fruit.

"Deaan Bowyer," said the leader of our captors (I later learned that 'deaan' was the honorific title for a king). "These men are from the ship that was sighted entering the bay. They came to the northern fort in a small party. The rest of them remain aboard their vessel."

"*Deaan* Bowyer?" said Walters, peering at the bedraggled king upon his throne of silk. "*Tom* Bowyer?"

The man's bristly eyebrows knotted as he focused his gaze on Walters. "George Walters?" he exclaimed. He looked to my other companions. "And I see Rogers and Harrison among you. The others I do not know."

"This is Captain Tomkinson of the *Azrael*," said Walters. "It is his ship your men saw in the bay. What has happened here, Bowyer? Why are the forts unmanned? And where is everybody else? All I see are natives ..."

"Natives, aye!" said Bowyer. "Born and bred to this land with white fathers and black mothers! What did you think we were doing with our time here?"

Walters looked to the mulatto warriors that had brought us before their king. "Do you mean to say these fellows are ..."

"My sons, aye, and the sons of many of our shipmates. We trade with King Andriamandisoarivo to the south and many of us took black wives, several to a man for so is the custom here!"

"Where is the rest of the colony?"

"Most have died of disease or violence, either at the hands of the Malagasy or their own mates. Some left and found new lives with the people to the east and the south. Only eleven of us remain."

"Eleven! Of over a hundred!"

Bowyer struggled to lift himself into an upright position, his two attendants falling away from him. "This is a harsh land! We faced starvation and slaughter by the Malagasy, not to mention our own quarrels which claimed many lives. Through hard fighting and careful alliances were we able to survive. That was our lot after being marooned by *you*!"

"That was Avery's doing," said Walters. "We knew nothing of it until we were far from Madagascar."

"I'm sure!" Bowyer sneered. "Along with most of the treasure! Many a night have we dreamed of our vengeance!"

"Then it will please you to know that Avery died in poverty, swindled out of the last of his diamonds by a pair of conmen in Bristol."

"And you? Why have you returned after all these years, along with your new friends?"

"We had hoped to find Libertatia still in operation," said Walters. "A trading outpost, a haven for men of fortune, not this ..." he glanced around at our surroundings, "this ... *squalor*!"

Bowyer grinned, revealing a mouth of blackened and broken teeth. "You came back here for the rest of the treasure! By the look of your ragged clothes, you squandered the loot you took from here and now you think to replenish your purses! No doubt you were well pleased to find us still here but did not expect to find our circumstances so changed!"

"Then Avery's treasure *is* still here?" said Captain Tomkinson. "You haven't bartered it all away with the blacks?"

Bowyer's eyes darted dangerously to him. "Oh, yes. *Our* treasure is still here. The Malagasy don't care for coin or diamonds. Guns is what they want, and beads and looking glasses. The treasure is still here, little good it does us. Or you, for that matter!"

"What do you mean?" Walters demanded.

"Libertatia is a civilised nation now," said Bowyer. "And traitors will face justice! Tomorrow you will stand trial." He barked an order to his warriors in the native tongue and we found ourselves being marched out of the blockhouse, prodded with spear tips every step of the way.

"What are you doing, Bowyer?" Walters cried. "We're your shipmates! In Avery's day, Libertatia offered hospitality to fellow men of fortune!"

"Avery is dead!" Bowyer could be heard cackling. "And Libertatia is mine!"

We were led across the compound to a stout wooden hut and shoved inside. The door was bolted behind us, locking us within the sweltering darkness.

Captain Tomkinson raged at our captors, explaining to them in highly colourful language what would happen to them once his crew realised we had been taken captive. He swore they would storm the settlement and butcher every one of them. I think even he knew the futility of his words for not only was the crew of the *Azrael* outnumbered by the men under Bowyer's command, how would they even know where we had been taken? We spent the rest of the day arguing and grumbling, each party blaming the other for our predicament until the heat sapped our strength and all we could do was suffer in silence.

As night fell, a woman was brought to our hut bearing a platter of charred meat and a large calabash of water. She was young and her hair was bound into buns on either side of her head. We tucked in ravenously and each took great gulps from the calabash before passing it on to the next man.

"Compliments of my mistress," said the woman.

"And who is your mistress?" I asked her.

"She is Kalobe, second wife of Deaan Bowyer."

"How many wives does he have?"

"Four. All the daughters of noblemen in the kingdoms to the south."

"And you? You have the skin of the Malagasy, not mixed with European blood like most people here."

"I am also from the south. I have been my mistress's slave since childhood. When Deaan Entwhistle captured her and forced her to be his wife, I was taken also."

"Deaan Entwhistle?"

"He was king of Libertatia before Deaan Bowyer slew him and took his kingdom and his wife as his own."

"I'm sure you mean old James Entwhistle," said Walters. "I remember him. A man of some standing in the old days. Doesn't surprise me that he ruled Libertatia after Avery's departure. So that's the way of it, eh? Tom Bowyer turned on his own shipmate and stole his wife."

"With the help of Toera, the village's holy man," the woman explained. "Together they plotted against Deaan Entwhistle. There was a terrible war. Many lost their lives in Deaan Bowyer's rebellion and any who resisted were captured and tied to a tree and shot through the heart."

"What is your name?" I asked the girl.

"My name is Rahena."

"You speak good English, Rahena."

"Thank you. My mistress had to learn the language of her husband and so too did I."

"Tell me, is it the custom among the Malagasy that their women are stolen and passed from man to man like chattel?"

"Not at all! But what choice does my mistress have? Deaan Bowyer rules Libertatia and we have no chance of escaping back to our people. If my mistress's father knew she still lived then perhaps he might aid us but ..."

"Do you mean to say that he believes her dead?"

"Many were killed in the uprising. Deaan Bowyer desired my mistress, you see. That is why he and Toera plotted against Deaan Entwhistle. He sent word to the south that she had been slain in the uprising. Now she is his forever."

"Has there been no opportunity for you and your mistress to escape?"

"None. We are prisoners here. My mistress is as the walking dead, her life stolen from her and her family ignorant of her existence."

"How far away are her people?"

"Deaan Andriamandisoarivo's lands lie sixteen miles to the south. But my mistress could never get away without being seen. Deaan Bowyer has her watched night and day."

The guard without the hut seemed angered at our conversation and demanded that Rahena be on her way. She left us then and left me with much to think about.

We were woken by much shouting in the village. With less than a few words of Malagasy between us, we were hardly able to decipher the cause of the ruckus, only that people were talking about a ship.

Rahena returned to us bearing a meagre breakfast of cold beef and goat's milk.

"What's all the shouting about?" I asked her around a mouthful of meat.

"Another ship arrived in the night," she said. "A big one that sits at anchor next to yours."

This caused much alarm among us. Another ship entering Narinda Bay when no ship had dropped anchor there in twenty years? It was too much to be a coincidence.

"You don't think it's the *Delicia*, do you?" Harrison asked.

"It's a fair bet," said Walters.

"How could they have followed us?"

"I don't know, but if I know Commander Rogers then he might have hung back on purpose and let us guide him to this place."

"How has Deaan Bowyer taken the news?" I asked Rahena.

"He is scared," she replied. "He thinks it is a British ship come to destroy him."

She was quickly called away and the guards began to haul us out, one by one. We were taken before Bowyer's house where almost the entire village had gathered in two columns with an avenue down the middle towards the door to the blockhouse. In front of it, a large baroque chair with tattered upholstery had been placed atop a wooden platform to form something of a throne. In the throne sat Deaan Bowyer, spear and rifle held ceremoniously in his hands. His wives also sat on the platform, two on either side and a collection of warriors whom I took to be his sons, were arrayed behind him, guns and shields in their hands. It was all so symbolic that I was sure that this was to be our trial.

"Strangers," Bowyer began. "When you arrived in my kingdom and I knew you to be some of the men who had marooned us so many years ago, I made up my mind on the spot that your sentence would be death."

"Damn you, Bowyer!" Walters raged. "It was always our intention to return here! But, after we bartered away the *Fancy* in New Providence so as to cover our tracks, we hadn't a ship to return in. We have spent some considerable time finding passage past the Cape."

"Aye, twenty years!" Bowyer bellowed. "I don't doubt that you sought to return, after each of you frittered away the wealth of two lifetimes! I know what it is you seek; that which haunted Avery night and day. But enough! You did not let me finish. I have decided to commute your sentence in the light of the circumstances we now find us in. Namely that bloody great frigate in the bay flying the flag of the East India Company."

We were silent, knowing now for certain that it was the *Delicia* that had entered the bay.

"There must be close to two-hundred men aboard her," Bowyer went on. "They could overrun us in a day. But with the rest of your crew ashore, we might man the forts and put up a considerable defence."

"So that's it," said Walters. "After imprisoning us and threatening us with death, you seek to use us to your advantage now that a threat to your little kingdom has arrived."

"It's a threat to us all," said Bowyer. "Or have you forgotten that there is a price on your head too? These East Indiamen won't care about our private squabbles. It's fight together or die apart now."

"You can't fight that ship," I said. "She has too many men and you don't know the man who commands her. We do."

Bowyer regarded me suspiciously. "How so?"

"That is the very ship that brought us here. She is called the *Delicia* and Woodes Rogers is her commander; a ruthless man who will stop at nothing to get what he wants. We jumped ship at St. Mary's but it seems that he has pursued us here. You cannot win against him."

"Then what do you suggest?" Bowyer snapped. "That I cower in my house and let him sweep aside all I have achieved here?"

"You can't beat him in battle and to fire the first shot would be folly. But we might be able to bargain with him. He's not a pirate hunter, you see. It's wealth he seeks, not justice for the Grand Mughal."

"He is a prize hunter?"

"My family knows him of old. He is a man in dire straits, and he outfitted the *Delicia* to find Avery's lost kingdom and its fabled riches. So far, I have yet to see a single piece of eight here but, if the treasure is no myth, then you might be able to buy him off with it."

Bowyer sat back in his throne, clearly not liking the idea of paying to get rid of a threat but I could see that he knew he was out of options.

"Let me be your go-between," I said. "Rogers knows me. I am sure I can reason with him."

I felt the eyes of my comrades upon me for neither they nor I were sure of any such thing. But I had to try for Bowyer seemed on the verge of opening fire on the *Delicia* and if that happened we would all be done for.

It took him a while but eventually the self-made king agreed and an expedition down to the shore was arranged. Bowyer was carried in a litter while the rest of us trudged alongside, led by a vanguard of Malagasy warriors. "I don't know you, lad," said Bowyer, as I walked alongside his litter. "You don't seem like much of a pirate to me and I don't know why you've thrown your lot in with Walters and those other scum. But I'd rather trust you than any of the others. Do right by me and I'll see to it that you will have a place here in Libertatia."

The fort had been occupied by Bowyer's men in the night, its gate repaired and the palisades bristled with spears and muskets. On the beach below, the men of the *Delicia* had camped, their longboats beached on the shore. So far, the peace was holding but I suspected only by a thread.

"Ahoy, down there!" Bowyer called, ascending the palisade above the gate.

Men stirred in the camp and I could see Woodes Rogers making his way to us. "Ahoy, the fort!" he cried.

"Why do you bar your gates to us? I was given to believe that Libertatia was a free republic and open to trade!"

"What makes you think you have landed at Libertatia?" Bowyer called back.

"Come, man!" Rogers replied. "No such settlement north of St. Augustine's Bay appears on any map! And I see deserters from my own ship at your side. They too sought Avery's lost kingdom and I followed in their wake. Whom am I addressing?"

"Thomas Bowyer is my name, and I am king of this place."

"Well, then, *King* Bowyer. We require food and fresh water and are willing to purchase both from you. Come, you would not refuse us?"

"Your men may camp on this shore," Bowyer replied. "And I will provide you with three beeves, with my compliments."

"Very gracious of you, Your Majesty. Allow me to offer you a barrel of rum from our hold."

The prospect of a fair trade seemed to cool the tension in the air. Once these gifts had been exchanged, there began to be talk of going aboard the *Delicia* to discuss terms.

"It has been many years since I trod an English deck," Deaan Bowyer said to Rogers.

"Well, come aboard and reacquaint yourself by all means," Rogers replied.

"Your men must remain here as surety for my safety. And I will bring some of my own with me."

"Of course."

I was chosen to join the party and several of the white men under Bowyer's command were keen to come too, sharing their leader's nostalgia for English oak under their feet. The twelve of us were as many men as Rogers was comfortable to have aboard and so, leaving Walters, Captain Tomkinson and the others ashore, we were ferried out to the *Delicia*; a ship I had no desire to be aboard again.

Two decades of life ashore showed immediately as we boarded for Bowyer and his lieutenants stumbled and rolled about like utter landlubbers and it struck me as a strange twist of fate that I, despite my inexperience of the sea, now had better sea legs than pirates who had sailed with Avery.

They spent a while marvelling at the fittings and quality of an East Indiaman before we were invited below for wine and talk.

"The *Delicia* is a fine ship," said Bowyer as he gulped the wine and wiped the red from his grey moustache with the back of his hand. "And this wine is better! By God, it has been many a year since I have tasted French wine!"

"You have suffered many depredations these years past," said Rogers. "How long since you have had contact with Christians?"

"Twenty," said Bowyer. "Twenty long years have we been the masters of this naked country; foraging, farming and trading with the savages since Avery betrayed us."

"Then this *is* Avery's lost kingdom?" Rogers asked, a sudden gleam in his eye. "This *is* the Libertatia spoken of in hushed whispers in the alehouses of England?"

Bowyer narrowed his eyes, surely sensing Rogers's keen interest. "Aye, this is Libertatia, founded by Avery during his red-handed exploits in the East Indies."

"Exploits in which you played your part as his crew?"

Bowyer looked around nervously with the face of one who senses a trap nearby.

Rogers chuckled. "Oh, I make no accusations. Avery is widely believed to be dead and I did not sail halfway across the globe to hunt down his old associates. My purpose in seeking out Libertatia was to bargain with its ruler whom I find to be you."

"Bargain?" Bowyer asked.

"There is a tale told," said Rogers as he lit his pipe in the manner of one who is about to embark on an old yarn, "that although Avery frittered away much of his fabulous wealth gained from robbing the Grand Mughal's fleet, there was one item he left behind in Libertatia for its value was so great that he knew he would never be able to sell it without raising the gravest suspicion."

"Oh?" said Bowyer, holding Rogers's stare.

"A diamond by the name of the Molucca Star cut from some Dutch East Indian mine. A diamond so large that it couldn't possibly be sold surreptitiously so it was left here, I assume, under your protection."

A smile began to form on Bowyer's face. "Oh, aye," he said. "The Molucca Star. That was indeed entrusted to my keeping."

Rogers was positively salivating at this. "Then it's really here?" he panted, as if he hadn't really believed in his own mission. "You have it?"

"Aye," said Bowyer, leaning back in his chair and swilling the last of his second glass of wine around in his hand. "I have it. The question is, what will you give me for it?"

"Well ..." said Rogers, trying to compose himself and recapture some of the cold authority he had possessed moments ago. "There is still a price on the heads of all of Avery's men. I have it within my power to make it go away."

I doubted that Rogers was speaking the truth. He was a penniless merchant funded by the East India Company. He didn't represent them and couldn't make decisions on their behalf. At best, he might put in a good word for Bowyer and his ten companions, but I doubted he would even go that far once he got that diamond in his hands.

"And if I don't give you the diamond, what will you do then, Commander Rogers?" Bowyer said with a testing smile.

"Oh, I make no threats," Rogers replied. "However, the intention of my voyage was well-known before I set out. Where I fail, others will surely pick up the hunt."

The threat, unspoken though it was, hung in the air between the two men.

"Very well," said Bowyer. "You shall have the diamond in return for full pardons for myself and every man of mine at this table as well as passage to England."

I might have been surprised by Bowyer's willingness to give in if I hadn't come to learn that he was just as conniving and wily as Rogers. A plan was forming in his head, I was sure of it. Whether Rogers suspected it was a different matter.

"Capital," said Rogers. "I will draw up the documents and you may have them as soon as you bring me the diamond."

"The diamond lies in Avery's old mansion some fourteen miles to the east," Bowyer said.

Rogers frowned. "Mansion?"

"Aye, or so he called it. In truth it is little more impressive than my own residence. He grew distrustful of his own people during his final days here and so built his own house in the wooded hills to the east. The place is abandoned now, home to nothing but the treasure he left behind."

"And you have not removed the treasure from that place to a more secure location?"

"What need have men of treasure without a ship to haul it? You may rest assured that the treasure is untouched. The natives have no interest in it and the place is treacherous to get to. I suggest a joint expedition. We may set out in the morning but tonight I invite you and your officers to a feast in my kingdom."

"Very good of you," said Rogers. "I will handpick several of my men and we shall set out in earnest at daybreak if that is agreeable to you?"

"*Capital*," said Bowyer with a smile.

I watched the exchange with a grim impotence. The Molucca Star, so sought after by my own shipmates, was now being handed over to Commander Rogers as payment for liberty. Bowyer and his men might get their pardons, but nothing had been said of pardoning myself and the other mutineers. We were not part of the deal.

Our business concluded aboard the *Delicia*, I was glad to return to land. Upon Bowyer's orders, the gates of the fort were thrown open to Rogers and his men who entered, eagerly anticipating the feast that was to come.

Walters, Captain Tomkinson and the others avidly awaited my report of what had occurred onboard the *Delicia*. You may well imagine their faces when I told them that the Molucca Star was practically in Rogers's pocket without us even setting eyes on it.

"And you just sat there and let Bowyer promise it to him?" Tomkinson raged at me.

"What precisely could I have done about it?" I snapped back at him. "We have nothing to bargain with and Bowyer does. We find ourselves rather unaffiliated in this mess."

Walters refrained from openly criticising me but made his frustrations plain all the same. "We haven't come halfway across the globe to be cheated out of what's rightfully ours!"

"The game isn't over yet," I told them. "Bowyer and Rogers aim to cheat each other, I am sure of it."

"How does that help us?" Tomkinson said.

"I don't know yet. Only that jackals must be ready to snatch what they can while two lions are at each other's throats."

Preparations for the feast began in earnest. None of us really knew what to expect but Bowyer's people seemed to understand exactly what was required and by the time the sun was setting, we found ourselves sitting by the light of the great cookfires with the smell of roasting beef in our nostrils.

Before we were served, a withered old Malagasy man dressed in some sort of ceremonial robes emerged from his hut bearing what looked to be a bundle of sticks, bones and brightly coloured cloth. As an attendant blew on a conch horn and the old man began to chant something in his own tongue, I became aware that some sort of ritual was taking place.

"What's all this?" I asked Rahena as she passed by.

"That is Toera, the holy man of the village," Rahena explained with a sour look in her eyes. "He is asking the ancestors of our people to bless the feast and the expedition tomorrow."

I frowned at the spry old goat who had helped Bowyer murder his way onto the throne of Libertatia. "What's that thing he's holding?"

"That is the *owley*. It is the sacred talisman of the village."

Two forked sticks were brought out and placed in the earth with a third resting upon them. The 'owley' was hung from this crossbeam and a fire was kindled beneath it. We watched in stunned silence as a white cow was brought forth and slaughtered. Deaan Bowyer was given a green bough which he dipped in the blood and flicked it on the owley. Hair and fat from the cow were tossed onto the fire, the smoke of which seemed to be considered beneficial to the talisman. The ceremony complete, the owley was whisked back into its hut by the old man.

The local cuisine prepared by Bowyer's people was beef roasted native style in the embers of the fire with the hair and skin still on as well as roasted yams and a sweet dish of tamarind paste which had been mixed with ash to take the sourness off. We drank the native drink of 'toaka' which is fermented honey and water very much like the mead of England and the great cask of rum that Rogers had given Bowyer was broken into. By the time the stars were out we were quite merry and Bowyer's men, having grown quite unused to rum, became exceedingly raucous.

Singing and dancing broke out and, amid the drunken revelry, Rahena slipped over to me and demanded that I follow her. Wary of some trick on the part of Bowyer, I followed cautiously as she led me away from the glow of the fires into the deep shadows between the huts. There I found Queen Kalobe waiting for me. I bowed low, my distrust and dislike of Bowyer having no effect on my opinion of his wife for she was indeed a beautiful and gracious woman. She wore a vivid silk lemba and her hair was done up in balls the size of hens' eggs.

"You are the one they call 'Rake'?" she asked, her English perfect but not unmarred by the accent of the common sailors who had taught her.

"I am, Your Majesty," I replied.

"We must speak quickly!" Rahena warned. "My mistress will be punished severely if Deaan Bowyer learns of this meeting."

"What can I do for you, Your Majesty?" I asked.

"My husband is lying to you," she said. "The diamond you seek is not in the house of Henry Avery. He is leading you and your countrymen into a trap."

I had suspected nothing less of a snake like Bowyer but now that his own wife had confirmed my suspicions, I was forced to try and think of a way out of it. "Where is the diamond?" I asked Kalobe.

"Right here in this village."

"Where?"

"That I do not know. My husband removed it from Avery's house after he killed Deaan Entwistle and took me for his own. I and the diamond were both his prizes, and he keeps us here behind his walls of thorns."

"But you don't know where he keeps the diamond? It's not in his house somewhere?"

93

"No, otherwise I would have seen it. I don't know where it is but that's not important. I'm sure he means to ambush you and the other Englishman on your journey tomorrow. He has given secret orders to his sons and they are preparing their warriors. I wish I knew more but he always keeps me in the dark. I have told you all I can and have risked much already."

"Thank you. But why have you helped me?"

"Because I am his prisoner and I hate him."

I could see the dull rage in her eyes; a fire dampened by the necessity to show obedience, but a fire that smouldered hot, nonetheless.

"You Englishmen are many," she said. "If you are prepared, you might overwhelm my husband and kill him. Then I will be free."

"It will be a bloody battle," I said. "And if we lose, things might be worse for you if your husband were to learn of your helping us."

"It is a risk I am willing to take."

Footfalls on the other side of the hut startled us and Rahena hurried her mistress to safety while I hovered in the shadows for a few moments before cautiously making my way back to the feast.

I didn't know what I was going to do. If the diamond was here in the village then the whole expedition tomorrow was pointless. But I could hardly make my excuses not to go for that would immediately arouse suspicion. No, I had to accompany Rogers and Bowyer to Avery's mansion and try to survive whatever trap Bowyer had planned for us. But that didn't mean I couldn't make a few plans of my own.

Once the feast had wound down and people started slumbering where they dropped, Walters, Tomkinson, the others and I made for a hut that had been put aside for our use as guests now that we were no longer prisoners. Once we were all inside and the door was shut, I told my companions of my secret audience with the queen.

"Vicious bastard!" Walters said. "He means to butcher us all and keep the diamond for himself, I'm sure of it!"

"Aye, and probably take our ships too," said Tomkinson. "He seems eager enough to return to England and with those pardons Rogers has drawn up for him, he likely has his heart set on a wealthy retirement!"

"He could take the *Azrael* easy enough," said Harrison, "but what of the *Delicia*?"

"It's within cannon range," I said. "And with Rogers ashore, he could press those onboard into surrendering."

"We're in a bind and no mistake," said Walters. "No diamond and soon enough, no ship! Bowyer will have us by the balls!"

"Not if we take the fort in his absence."

They all looked at me, their eyes wide in the moonlight that streamed in through the shutters.

"Most of Bowyer's warriors will be keeping pace with us tomorrow," I said.

"Leaving this village and the fort undefended," said Walters.

"Aye. And, if Kalobe is to be trusted, then the diamond is right here under our noses."

"We'll ransack the place while you are playing along with Rogers and Bowyer," said Walters.

"I'd rather you secured the fort and made sure those guns are trained on the *Delicia*," I said. "We need to make sure she stands away from the shore and gives us the chance to make it to the *Azrael*."

"Do you know exactly what Bowyer is planning to do?" Harrison asked.

"No. I'll just have to play it by ear but I'm hoping I'll be able to double back at some point, leaving Rogers to deal with Bowyer and his men."

"It's a bloody dangerous plan," said Walters.

I nodded. "But it's the only play we can make to my way of thinking."

It was a slower start than initially planned the following morning as Bowyer and his men had overindulged somewhat on the rum and were nursing sore heads. We got going a little before noon, each of us carrying a calabash of water and a pouch of charred meat, except Bowyer who had his slaves carry enough for him and his warriors. We were around twenty men in number; Bowyer and his attendants made up a little under half with Rogers and his men making up the rest with the addition of myself and Captain Tomkinson.

We trudged our way across the reddish hills beneath the baking heat of midday. The hills swept down into green valleys cut through by rivers and mangrove swamps. The vegetation became dense and we had to hack a path with our cutlasses. Bowyer's scouts led the way and, as dusk fell, reported that Avery's mansion lay a little to the northeast.

It sat upon a hill thick with thorny trees grown, as in Bowyer's village, as a defensive maze around the house. Bowyer's scouts knew the way into its interior but the way was so overgrown that we had to cut through it all the same.

The mansion itself was much in the style of Bowyer's residence and I supposed the same hands had built it. It was in poorer repair with mouldering thatch and foliage that grew thick around it, crawling up its walls like the tendrils of some great octopus with fan palms towering over all.

Upon entry, we found ourselves in a gloomy hall over which time had cast its severe gaze. Dust lay thick over everything, and the webs of spiders hung in the corners. Torches were brought in and the hearth fire was kindled for it was dark outside now and the moonlight did little to penetrate the gloom. Once we grew more aware of our surroundings, we began to see the glint of metal winking like cats' eyes in the blackness. We were surrounded by items of great value; too big to be carried away by Avery and so left to gather dust in this naked land where they had no value. Persian carpets covered the floors, oriental vases squatted in corners and boxes and chests of rich cloths, jewellery and coins of a hundred nations lurked in the shadows.

"Here it is, lads," Bowyer said, spreading his arms wide. "The spoils of a dozen lifetimes! Avery's treasure, paid for in blood!"

There was a crackle outside as of somebody treading on a dry twig.

"What was that?" one of Rogers's men asked.

"Somebody's outside!" said another, scurrying over to the window to peep out. "Malagasy!" he exclaimed. "Dozens of the buggers!"

"You had your men follow us," Rogers said to Bowyer.

Grinning, Bowyer moved towards the door, his attendants following him.

"What's the game, Bowyer?" Rogers asked. "Where are you going?"

"I am returning to my village," Bowyer replied. "You will remain here. You wanted Avery's treasure, well, here it is. You are welcome to it for Avery's house will be your tomb!"

"Hold it right there," said Rogers, drawing the pistol from his belt and pointing it at Bowyer.

This alarmed Bowyer's men and they unslung their muskets and aimed them at Rogers. In return, Rogers's men pointed their own weapons at Bowyer's men. The only ones in the room not pointing a gun at somebody was Tomkinson and myself.

"Did you really think I wouldn't have prepared for your treachery?" Rogers asked Bowyer.

"Killing me will hardly serve your cause," said Bowyer. "My men surround this place. There is no escape for you."

Rogers put his fingers to his lips and let out a sharp whistle. As if in reply, three gunshots sounded from somewhere in the darkness beyond the house. The eyes of Bowyer's men darted about in sudden uncertainty.

"I also had my men follow us," said Rogers. "Or follow your own men, rather. I knew you'd try to trick us somehow, your mind no doubt set on taking my ship. Well, you've got more than you bargained for with me, Bowyer. Now, where is the Molucca Star?"

"Its location hardly serves you now," said Bowyer with one of his rotten-toothed grins. "But if you'd really like to know, it is far from here."

Rogers's face seethed. "You led us on a wild goose chase, then."

"Aye. You really think I'd leave that diamond here with the dust and cobwebs? Oh, I know I said that Avery's treasure does us no good here in Madagascar, but that diamond has a value more important than mere wealth. It is the very keystone of Avery's kingdom. He didn't just leave it here for safekeeping. He left it here as if it were his own heart, useless to him anywhere else for its home was right here in Libertatia. He left it here so he might reclaim it one day. The diamond *is* Libertatia and whoever possesses it, possesses the kingdom!"

That last comment set a few wheels turning in my head I can tell you, but I knew that all rested on Tomkinson and myself getting out of that wolf's den alive.

There were more gunshots outside and, the nervousness of Rogers's men distracting them, Bowyer was able to get the upper hand and make a run for the door. Rogers's pistol flashed and the ball slammed into the doorpost as Bowyer exited the house. His men fired in reply and two of Rogers's men were struck.

Tomkinson and I had flung ourselves low, our pistols in our hands, not knowing what to do. Rogers had taken cover behind the dining table and was reloading. His men were firing back at Bowyer's lads who blocked the doorway.

"The window!" Tomkinson hissed to me. "We can get out that way!"

Although Rogers seemed to have forgotten our presence, I had no doubt that he would shoot us in the back if he spotted us trying to escape. Keeping low, we shuffled over to the window. I let Tomkinson heave his great bulk up and through it first, sweeping the room with my pistol to cover his wide arse. When it was my turn, I shoved my pistol in my belt and wriggled through, tumbling down into the prickly foliage on the other side.

We hurried across the overgrown compound feeling horribly naked in the silver moonlight. We could see occasional flashes of orange light signifying the ongoing battle between Bowyer's and Rogers's men at the entrance which, unfortunately, was our only way out.

We kept to the shadows of the tall, spiny hedge that circled the house as we worked our way towards the gap. We could see figures hurrying about, occasionally illuminated by the flash of gunpowder. The battle seemed to be mostly concentrated around the house's entrance with the Malagasy keeping Rogers inside and Rogers's men pressing the assault against them. We found the entrance to the compound deserted and thanked our stars as we slipped through and began the long, winding way through the maze of hedges.

Neither of us quite remembered the way for these things are constructed by the Malagasy to confuse enemies and it did a fine job of confusing us. Twice we argued that we had already passed a certain spot and the fear that we were going around in circles only deepened our desperation.

The sound of running feet approaching from the interior threw us into a panic and we got down into the dirt and tried to squeeze ourselves beneath the thorny bushes, their spines jabbing us painfully. A troop of Malagasy hurried past us on some errand, their bare feet drumming on the earth. I wondered if this meant that Rogers and his men were dead and that the battle was over but, in this maze, we couldn't be sure if they were coming or going.

The danger seemingly passed, we scrambled out of our hiding place and tried not to yelp as we pulled the thorns from our flesh before continuing. The ground which had recently dipped down began to rise again and I fancied that we were out of the maze and into the forest for the land was so tangled that it was difficult to make a distinction between the two. Now all we had to do was head south-west until we found Bowyer's village or, failing that, the coast.

A gunshot cracked the still night air behind us and Tomkinson, giving up a cry, threw his arms above his head and tumbled back down the hill, a ball lodged in his back. I cursed and hurried on, ignoring the cries of the Malagasy behind us. A second gunshot sent a ball whizzing past me and I kept my head low as I wove my way through the trees.

I had crested the hill and it began to slope away at a much steeper grade. I found my legs carrying me at an alarming rate and I nearly tumbled headlong before I was able to gain control by grasping at trunks and branches. I knew I was being pursued and I knew that I could never outrun these Malagasy who were native to this land that I was so alien to. My only hope was to find someplace to hide.

I found myself on the edge of the mangrove swamp we had passed on the way to Avery's mansion and I was glad to know that I was at least headed in the right direction. I waded into the water and pulled myself beneath the roots of a mangrove, trying not to splash about too much. I could hear the voices of the Malagasy as they passed close to my position and I held my breath as they faded away.

Too afraid to emerge from my hiding place in case they were still in the vicinity, I waited there in the dank water between the slimy roots for several hours until my fear of the crocodiles outweighed my fear of the Malagasy. The day was breaking when I clambered out of that swamp and I knew I had a hard trot ahead of me. I set off at once, the rising sun baking the mud hard on my clothes.

I found the occasional stream on the way and was able to relieve my thirst but the sun was high in the sky by the time I could see the palisade and thorny enclosure of Bowyer's village. I imagine I looked like some primal beast as I approached: torn, ragged and coated in dried mud. There was a cry from some sentry and the gate was opened to let me in. I was greeted by Walters and was pleased to see that the men had not been idle in my absence. Everybody was armed and the women and children cowered in their huts, occasionally peeping out.

"What the devil happened to you?" Walters exclaimed, looking me up and down.

"Bowyer's treachery, that's what," I said. "I barely escaped with my life. Tomkinson didn't. They shot him in the back as we ran."

The crew of the *Azrael* looked dismayed at this.

"What of Rogers and Bowyer?" Walters asked.

"Slain each other for all I care," I replied. "I left them in a pitched battle. But never mind them now, what goes on here?"

"We've taken the village, as you can see, and I've sent Harrison and Rogers and a couple of men from the

Azrael to prepare the guns at the fort. But what of the diamond? We've ransacked the place but short of razing it to the ground, I'm blowed if I know where Bowyer has squirreled it away. I don't want to leave here without it but how long do we have? Should we expect many of Bowyer's warriors to return? Or the men from the *Delicia* for that matter?"

"We have time enough," I said. "Where is Queen Kalobe and Rahena?"

"In the hut of that old coot along with Bowyer's other wives."

"The holy man?"

"Aye. He's probably offering some sort of spiritual protection to the king's family."

"Did you search the place?"

"We did. There's not much there though. It's a shrine to their ancestors or so I believe."

"Follow me." I turned and headed towards the small hut.

We found the wives of Deaan Bowyer huddled around the hearth along with their attendants and their children. Kalobe was there, but I could not see her handmaiden anywhere.

"Where is Rahena?" I asked Kalobe.

"I sent her on an errand," Kalobe replied.

"What sort of errand?" The queen did not answer and I turned to Walters. "Did you let Rahena leave the village?"

"I was not aware that she was missing," he replied. "It's possible she snuck off during the confusion."

I regarded Kalobe's unreadable face, trying to see what she was up to but I was diverted by an angry outburst from Toera the priest.

"He demands that you leave this sacred place at once," Kalobe translated for us. "Your presence here offends the spirits of our ancestors."

"Tell him that we are in charge of this village now," I said, "and tell him he'd better settle down and not cause us any bother."

Kalobe did not need to translate my words to the holy man for he either understood English or he took my meaning plain enough. This set him off on another raging fit and he jabbed at me with his knotted staff as if he planned to club me senseless with it. I considered drawing my pistol on him to convince him that I wasn't fooling around but our exchange was interrupted by cries from outside.

We hurried out and found our sentries in a panic. Men were approaching, they said. *Malagasy warriors.*

"Bowyer and his followers have returned?" I asked.

"No," one pirate replied. "Too many of them for that. And these are no half-breeds. This looks to be another tribe!"

"That's all we need!" said Walters. "Another bunch of them taking advantage of the situation. Man the palisades! We'll see if we can't parlay with them."

"These men do not come to parlay," said Kalobe, appearing at my side. "They come for vengeance."

"How do you know?" I asked her.

"Because it is my father and brothers. I sent for them."

My jaw dropped and I scrambled up the ladder to the top of the palisade. Over a hundred Malagasy warriors were hacking and burning their way through the thorny barricades. Through the plumes of smoke and wavering heat I could see a finely dressed Malagasy with much gold and silver ornamentation bellowing orders at his men. At his side stood Rahena gazing in our direction.

"You sent Rahena to inform your father that you are alive!" I said to Kalobe as I climbed back down the ladder.

"Yes," she replied.

"And now he'll kill anyone in his path to get you back."

"That's the idea. My husband may be dead or he may not be. But I take no chances. When your men took over the village I was suddenly free to do that which I have longed to do for over a year. Rahena ran all night but she carried my message to my people and now they have come for me."

I did not begrudge the queen for taking her opportunity but it certainly put us in a bit of a tight spot. Her people were coming to destroy the white men who had held her captive and I doubted they would stop to differentiate between us and Bowyer's men. We had to accelerate our plans and get off Madagascar as quickly as possible.

The remaining inhabitants of Bowyer's kingdom were thrown into a panic by the attack, their fear no doubt compounded by the fact that their king was missing along with almost every one of their warriors. They ran back and forth, gathering belongings and loved ones to them. There was no thought given to defending their village, only for escape. With King Andriamandisoarivo attacking from the south, an escape route was left open to the north but, as the thorny barricades surrounded us on all sides, the village's defences had become its prison.

Pirates and Malagasy worked together in tearing down a section of the palisades and men with blades filled the breach, hacking a path through the barricades. Walters ordered a detachment of pirates to the southern palisade where they attempted to hold off the advancing warriors with musket fire. I made my way back to Toera's hut.

"Where the devil are you going?" Walters demanded.

"To get that diamond!" I called back.

I found the hut deserted. Bowyer's wives no longer counted on the spirits of the ancestors for safety and were no doubt fleeing north along with the rest of the village. In the middle of the chamber, upon its stone pedestal, sat the owley of Libertatia.

I snatched it up and peered into it. In its centre, nestled amid crocodile's teeth, bundles of sticks and bright cloth, something twinkled like the glistening egg of an exotic bird.

"You must not touch the sacred owley!" screamed a heavily accented voice to the left of me. Toera emerged from where he had been cowering in the shadows, his face hateful and his bony fists gripping his ceremonial staff.

"So you *can* speak English," I said.

Before I could draw my pistol he was upon me, swinging savagely with his weapon.

I dropped the owley and grasped Toera's staff with both hands and tried to rip it out of the old man's grip but he was stronger than his frail form credited. Spitting curses at me in his native tongue, he forced me towards the pedestal, bending me back over it.

A face appeared at Toera's right shoulder. It was Kalobe, her dark eyes fixed on the holy man's head with grim determination. Toera gasped in sudden agony and I realised that Kalobe had slipped a knife into his back.

His arms hung slack and the staff clattered to the floor. He stumbled backwards, reaching impotently for the hilt of the knife that was beyond his reach. He collapsed, the death rattle escaping his lips, to lie still on the floor.

"Thank you, Your Majesty," I said to Kalobe. "That old man was more powerful than he looked."

"His evil plotting is at an end," the queen said, not taking her eyes off the body at our feet. "No longer shall he poison minds and pit king against king."

I picked up the owley and reached inside it. My hands grasped the diamond and I ripped it free causing the talisman to fall apart in my hands.

"Sorry," I said to Kalobe. "About the owley."

"It does not matter. It is already defiled by Toera's wickedness," she said. "He and my husband used it for great evil. Their kingdom dies with it."

We left the hut and found the village practically deserted. Only Walters and the brave few pirates who manned the palisades remained but now they had left their posts and were hurrying across the compound. King Andriamandisoarivo's warriors had reached the palisades and were scrambling over them.

"Quickly!" Walters said as he ran towards us. "We must make for the boats. White skin is a death sentence in this place now!"

"Will you be all right?" I asked Kalobe.

"I will be fine," she replied. "The stain of my husband has been removed from this place. Tomorrow it will be razed to the ground. I am free."

I nodded in reply, no suitable parting words coming to mind. I knew this was to be the last I would see of her. I joined Walters and the remaining pirates as they dashed towards the gap in the northern wall.

The whoops and cheers of the victors seared the air behind us, peppered with the sound of muskets being fired in jubilation. We hadn't even covered half the distance to the fort before we realised that we were being pursued.

"By God, they mean to butcher us all!" Walters panted as he glanced over his shoulder.

"Let's just hope Rogers and the others have those guns ready," I said. "The last thing we need is the *Delicia* impeding our escape."

We scrambled up the slope leading to the fort, knowing that the Malagasy were closing on our heels. As we entered the fort's compound, Rogers scrambled down from the gun platform.

"What the bloody hell have you stirred up, Rake?" he demanded, looking past us at the approaching Malagasy.

"Not us," I said. "No time to explain. Have you got those guns primed?"

"Aye, but there's no need for them. The *Delicia* has gone upriver. They passed us not half an hour ago. We reckon they spotted the smoke inland and are headed in to see what's going on."

"Feared for the life of their commander," said Walters.

"Well, that's a boon to us," I said. "Now, to the boats!"

I was glad to find that an extra longboat from the *Delicia* was beached alongside our own from the *Azrael* and assumed it belonged to the men Commander Rogers had snuck ashore the previous night. Even so, both boats were barely adequate to ferry all of us out to the *Azrael* and they rode perilously low in the water. With the oarsmen tugging for all they were worth, we made slow progress across the bay.

"Look!" Walters cried out, pointing back at the shore. "The Malagasy have the fort!"

Turning my head, I could make out several black figures climbing to the gun platform. "By God, they'll bring those guns to bear on us!" I immediately regretted sending Rogers and the others to prime them for now we were their target, not the *Delicia*.

Sure enough, the whistle of a cannonball overhead preceded the delayed 'boom' of a nine pounder. The shot sent up a spray of water not three yards from our larboard bow. We all ducked instinctively, causing the boat to rock and reel.

"Keep her steady!" I yelled to the oarsmen. "And pull for your bloody lives!"

Two more shots roared past, dousing us in salty spray. Men began to pray. The oarsmen heaved so that the sweat ran down their faces and their muscles knotted.

Another shot thundered out, this time louder and closer.

"It's the *Azrael*!" Walters cried. "She's firing back!"

Our pirate ship had come about and was aiming her bow chasers at the fort. Another puff of smoke sent a second ball whickering over our heads and we gave up a cheer as we saw it strike the gun platform, sending great splinters of wood up in the air.

"Whoever is in charge of those gun crews shall have my rum ration tonight!" Walters cried.

We had no more trouble from the fort as we came alongside the *Azrael* and the boats were hoisted up. Orders were immediately given to get out of range of the fort and make for the open sea. I was not the only one glad to see Libertatia – or whatever was left of Avery's dream – vanish as we passed the headland and headed out into the Mozambique Channel.

Once we were underway and rounding the northern tip of Madagascar, Walters, Rogers, Harrison, Solomon and I gathered around the captain's table in the Great Cabin and inspected the Molucca Star. I had placed it on the table and we stood in awe of its brilliance, marvelling at the way it reflected the light of the table lamp.

"By God, we'll all be as rich as kings once that thing is sold," I said.

"As to that," said Walters, "we have a task ahead of us greater than getting hold of the bloody thing. We can't just sail to England and try and flog it there. Not without having to answer some very difficult questions."

"How the hell are we going to sell it then?" I asked.

"There are other places."

"Such as?"

"The Caribbean has its share of merchants who can shift certain items without raising too much suspicion. And we have plenty of contacts in those waters."

"It must stay hidden in the meantime," I said, "and we must not breathe a word of it to the rest of the crew."

"Aye," said Rogers. "Tomkinson's crew are good lads but this is the sort of treasure that a cove might find a shipmate's knife in his back over."

"Only the men in this cabin know of what we recovered from Libertatia," I said. "We need to keep it that way, agreed?"

The others voiced their agreement and I placed the diamond in a lockbox which we then stowed under the captain's table. It was agreed that I would keep the key as I had proven my trustworthiness in the past few days and was looked on well by my new companions.

I had much to think over as we put into Bourbon to resupply and careen the badly fouled hull of the *Azrael*. Even though I missed Bristol and called no other place home, I had nothing left there. Besides, I was a mutineer and the law would lump me in with Walters and the others if it could get its hands on me. But was I ready to throw my lot in with pirates and sail with them to the West Indies? Once a man sets his foot on that path, there is no going back, and I knew I might never tread Bristol's streets again.

We spent some very idle days on Bourbon once the *Azrael* was careened and enjoyed the respite after our ordeals in Madagascar. We were about fifty men in all, most having been part of Captain Tomkinson's crew. Talk of sailing to the West Indies was rife and there also began to be talk of voting in a captain.

Walters was the obvious choice as leader of the small band of Avery's old followers and there was nobody of much authority in Tomkinson's crew, but I was surprised to find that my name was also being put forward.

"It was your plan to take the village while Bowyer was away," Walters explained to me one night while we lay in the shade of a lean-to, sipping rum. "The men also admire your courage in going along on that expedition to Avery's mansion. And, as far as I'm concerned, you will forever have my thanks for getting us off the *Delicia* in the first place. None of us would be here if it wasn't for you. You show leadership, brains and courage and that's pretty much all there is to it when it comes to captaining."

"What about seamanship?" I asked. "I'm still something of a landlubber."

"That's what a crew is for," he replied. "With experienced hands beneath him, a captain doesn't need to know much of how to sail a ship."

I was flattered by this old sea rogue's opinion of me. Although I had often been the one coming up with the schemes in those old days in Bristol, I had never considered myself much of a leader. Yet here I was, held in high regard by fifty hardened but unorganised pirates who needed a captain to forge them into a proper crew. My longing for England was outweighed by the temptation such a prospect held. I wasn't ignorant of the dangers a pirate's occupation held but I'd be lying if some romantic streak in me was not tempted by the prospect of adventure.

The following morning the vote was held and I was chosen as the *Azrael*'s captain with Walters as quartermaster. I felt that my future had been laid before me and I no longer had any thoughts of returning to

England. I was twenty-two years old and captain of a pirate crew on my way to the West Indies.

PART 3 – NASSAU AND THE VIRGIN ISLANDS, SPRING TO SUMMER, 1715

Our voyage east was long and toilsome. We made good time around the Cape of Good Hope and up the western coast of Africa but once we put out across the Atlantic, I found myself overawed by the enormity of the ocean. Weeks passed with no change in the endless expanse of blue. My companions worked through it with admirable cheer, seemingly oblivious to my mounting distress even as we entered the dreaded doldrums where the wind failed us, and our sails hung slack for days on end. I knew our destination lay out there somewhere, but I could not escape the uneasy feeling that we were drifting on into infinity, too far from land now to make it back on our dwindling stores.

I tried to distract myself by learning everything there was to be learned from my crew. With many able-bodied seamen like Walters, the combined knowledge aboard the *Azrael* was surely enough to turn even an incompetent landlubber like myself into a master mariner. And time was one thing we were not short on. Walters took me on as his pupil and did his best to teach me the ins and outs of captaincy including charting a course and puzzling out latitude and longitude.

I even took instruction from some of the other battle-hardened pirates on swordsmanship and many an afternoon rang with the clash of steel as I practiced feints, parries and attacks from one end of the deck to the other. I must confess that I enjoyed these lessons more than Walters' lectures in navigation. The streets of Bristol had bred me to be a brawler and I much prefer the hot-blooded fight to studying charts and fiddling with sextants.

It was in the early months of 1715 that we finally put in at the port of Nassau on New Providence Island. You will no doubt have heard of the place for it is the very cradle of piracy in the Caribbean. All the great buccaneers you care to name; Thache, Hornigold, Jennings, Vane, Rackham and myself, we all got our start in that degenerate cesspool of villainy which we flatteringly called the 'capital' of our pirate republic.

It was Walters who put Nassau forward as our destination. He had gone there with Avery in 1695 after they had deserted their comrades in Madagascar. Even back then it had been a fairly lawless place, technically a British colony but largely ignored by the Royal Navy.

"The governor in those days was a man by the name of Nicholas Trott," Walters told me. "A corrupt sod but they make the most useful associates. We bribed him with a hefty sum as well as the *Fancy* itself including its cargo of elephant tusks and slaves which we had picked up en route. For that, he let us have the run of the place and lied to the island's council that we were just unlicensed slavers looking to lay low for a while. The council were keen to have us, you see, for our presence and the guns of the *Fancy* provided some security in the face of French attack which eventually did come, though we were long gone by then."

"Why did you leave?" I asked Walters.

"Trott couldn't keep his end of the bargain. The East India Company got wind of our presence in the Bahamas. Probably the *Fancy* had been seen or perhaps folk had got curious about the foreign coinage we were spending. As they closed in on Nassau, Trott couldn't pretend ignorance anymore and was forced to put out a warrant for Avery's arrest. He warned us ahead of time and we made our preparations to leave. Trott dashed the *Fancy* on the rocks of Hog Island to cover up his association with us.

"That's when the last of Avery's crew broke up for good. Most went north for the Carolinas. Avery and two score or so, myself included, returned to England. Carelessness and treachery did for most of them and five met their end at Execution Dock with a dozen or so more acquitted by the skin of their teeth. Avery was swindled out of what was left of his fortune as I told you, and the rest of us vanished into obscurity.

"As for Nassau, God alone knows what goes on there now. A lawless pirates' nest by all accounts, abandoned by the British after attacks by the French and Spanish. The younger men in the crew say that a man called Benjamin Hornigold rules the roost now and that he controls trade in the Bahamas. They put much stock in him and if we are to make something of ourselves in the West Indies, then it is to him that we must present ourselves."

Upon my first visit to Nassau, and upon that time only, I saw it for what it was. I think everybody does. I saw only the gatherings of semi-permanent tents made from sailcloth and palmetto poles clustered around smouldering bouccan fires. Rag-tag bands of drunken pirates swaggered about, dicing and whoring and the place had a decidedly unhealthy stink to it. The town above the beach was little better. Ramshackle and grubby clapboard buildings clung for purchase against the ever-encroaching jungle like barnacles in the shadow of Nassau's crumbling fort. This is all Nassau seemed to be upon my first impressions; a diseased and wretched infestation that awaited only the guns of the British or the Spanish to wipe it away for good.

Then I met Benjamin Hornigold.

We were led to the old fort where the pirate lord had made his residence and, as we passed through the squalid dwellings of the beach and town, Walters looked about with a distaste that matched my own.

"What the bloody hell has become of the place?" he exclaimed as a flea-bitten dog scampered between two buildings with a piece of offal in its jaws, pursued by two similar mongrels who would no doubt fight to the death for the morsel of rancid meat.

"Is it much changed since your last visit?" I asked him.

"Aye, you could say that. It was never much of a place in the old days, but it has grown tenfold since I left. And every bugger here is a scoundrel of some sort or I'm a French washerwoman."

The fort was in about as poor a state as the town. Gun placements had been stripped, nobody stood guard and it seemed to be little more than a shell of a place, pockmarked and shattered by Spanish cannonballs. If anybody had half a mind to take Nassau they could walk right up and knock.

We climbed the stairs to the terreplein where we found Benjamin Hornigold sunning himself in a wicker chair, fanned by the palms of two black men. He was a man in his middle years with greying side whiskers and wore the plain clothes of a navy man. I don't know what I had expected. Perhaps more gold ornamentation or luxurious silks. Whatever my idea of how the ruler of

Nassau and its pirate crews should have looked, Benjamin Hornigold struck me as rather understated.

"New captain come to pay his respects, sir," said the man who had led us into the fort. "Captain Rake of the ... what was it, lad?"

"The *Azrael*," I said, trying to inject as much importance into the name as possible.

"Indeed?" Hornigold said turning in his chair to look us up and down, paying especial attention to me. "Captain Rake is it? I have not heard the name."

"Philip Rake, sir," I said, laying on the respect I felt the situation warranted. "We are recently come from Madagascar and seek to make our fortunes in the West Indies."

"Hmm. I detect the whiff of the West Country in your voice, Rake. Where is it you call home?"

"Bristol, sir."

"A fellow Englishman. I'm from Norfolk myself but more and more men from your end of the country are popping up in Nassau. Good seafaring folk."

I said nothing, not wanting to let on that I was far from what he might consider 'good seafaring folk'.

"How many men do you have?" he asked.

"We number fifty-odd," I said. "But we hope to pick up more hands soon. The *Azrael* is a fine brig, if in need of a few modifications and some more guns."

"You won't find many hands in Nassau at this time of year," Hornigold said. "Most of my captains are out chasing prizes at present. You'll have more luck once the hurricane season starts and they all put in for the autumn. You are aware of the weather patterns in the West Indies?"

"Aye, my quartermaster and some of my crew have been here before," I said. "Walters here was part of Avery's crew and he's not the only one."

That impressed Hornigold just as I had hoped it would. He glanced at Walters and appraised him with his beady eyes. "Henry Avery, eh? You must have some tales to tell. I'd like to hear them over a pot of bumbo one night."

"I'd be happy to oblige as long as you're not hoping to learn from me where Avery buried his treasure," Walters said. "I can tell you now that it was all squandered away along with Avery's life. Legend can tell the tall tales it wants to but I can give you a more reasonable account of Henry Avery."

Hornigold smiled. "Done. Well, then, you seem like a likely crew and I'd be glad to have you aboard my little enterprise. We call ourselves the Flying Gang on account of how we can swoop out of these islands and take what we want before vanishing just as quick. Nassau is well-hidden and close enough to the trade routes. Here we sit pretty and make ourselves rich but everybody must pull his own weight. I have few rules, but I am a stickler for two. Firstly, you prove yourselves to be good earners. Fifteen percent of all prizes must be handed over to me to invest in the security of this place. Secondly, no member of the Flying Gang is to attack British ships. I hope that a fellow Englishman can appreciate my dedication to this last point."

"No attacking British ships?" I exclaimed, putting voice to the concerned murmuring of my crew. "What sense is there in that? I was given to believe that men who had made Nassau their home were outcasts, cut off from their homelands. Enemies to all nations. Surely the

British ships heading back to Europe with rum and molasses from Jamaica are the fattest prizes of all?"

"We have a good spot here in Nassau," said Hornigold, his voice matching his face in its severity. "But our survival depends on keeping out of the shadow of the Royal Navy. How long do you think we would last if we started taking British ships? They would renew their interest in the Bahamas and there would be precious little we could do to stop them from reclaiming them. Then it would be the gibbet for all of us. It is not patriotism that lies behind this rule, Rake, but survival. One day we will be strong enough to take on the British but for now we take Spanish and French prizes but not British. Am I understood?"

"I see the sense in your caution," I agreed, somewhat reluctantly for I knew my crew would take some persuading on this point. "But refusing to attack British ships will only keep you safe from the British. What of the Spanish? How do you intend to defend this place should they take an interest in how you are running things here? I haven't seen a single gun in this fort. In fact, the place looks like a ruin."

I felt the others tense at my side and I knew I was probably mouthing off at the wrong time but, truth be told, if we were going to have to join this rag-tag outfit, then I felt we had a vested interest in the security of it all.

Hornigold fixed a sly eye on me and sucked on his pipe. Then, he broke into a grin. "By God, sir!" he exclaimed. "You are a stripling of a lad but you speak with a man's tongue in your head! Fine, fine! I don't mind an inquisitive chap who isn't afraid to speak up when he feels something is amiss. You are quite right,

Captain Rake, there is but a single nine-pounder in this fort. Hardly enough to repel a Spanish sloop let alone one of their men-of-war. But we are quite safe here for the time being, I assure you. Come!"

He got up from his chair and beckoned me to follow him to the tip of the bastion that jutted out over the rocks below. "See Hog Island across the bay?" he said.

I looked over at the long, low island that shielded Nassau's harbour from end to end. "Aye," I said.

"That island is our barricade. The eastern entrance to the bay is too shallow to allow entry to anything larger than a fourth-rate ship of the line. And the western entrance is gated by a sand bar that reaches out from the island like a curved finger. The entrance there is a mere two cables long and this fort, once I get it up and running, will easily cover it with its guns. So you see, my dear Captain Rake, we are quite safe here. Nevertheless, I forbid the taking of British ships, at least for the time being."

Hornigold seemed keen to convince people that one day his order might be rescinded, and the Flying Gang would be permitted to prey on the British. Perhaps he needed to hold this promise over his gang to keep them in line. I still wasn't convinced that the order was born of the need for survival alone and that he did not retain some sense of patriotism, pirate king he might be.

We re-joined the others and Hornigold called for rum to be brought. We toasted ourselves and the Flying Gang. Hornigold told us of the other captains and their crews and the large scores they had recently hauled in, partly by way of boasting but partly, I suspect, to set the standard for us. There was no mistake; we were to earn our keep.

"I have asked each captain that has set out this season to keep a weather eye out for any unusual Spanish activity," he told us. "Since us British privateers made these waters too hot for them during the recent war, they have held off sending their treasure fleets back to Spain. The gold and silver has been piling up in Havana like gull shit below a cliff! From what we have gathered, they are preparing to send the largest treasure fleet that has ever put out from the New World and they plan to send it this summer."

"And you want to know exactly when it leaves so you might ... attack it?" I asked incredulously. "Such a fleet would have an escort too powerful for even the Flying Gang, surely?"

"You are right there, Captain Rake," said Hornigold despondently. "But there are always stragglers, ships that fall behind, get separated from the fleet. Just one of those treasure ships would secure our little republic here for good and all. We need only be ready as wolves to swoop in and take the fallen lamb. So, my bully boys! Learn what you can from the Spaniards once you put out. Any prize, no matter how small, may carry word of when this bloated fleet intends to set out."

We spent a week or so in Nassau resupplying and enjoying the pleasures that were to be had. There were plenty of trollops plying their trade and there was even a brothel where my crew gladly spent what little coin they had. Personally, I had little interest in women. Every toss of perfumed hair and every white bosom made me think of Mary Read and all I had left behind in Bristol. I found myself thinking of her often and wondering if she was happily married to her haberdasher in Surrey. Despite their relationship being the root of my downfall, I hoped that it was so.

We got to know some of the other captains of the Flying Gang and I was surprised at the lack of rivalry between the various crews for I had always thought of pirates as a quarrelsome lot. But there seemed to be a sense of community despite the squalor and drunkenness that permeated the settlement. I gradually came to admit that this Flying Gang might be a force to be reckoned with and its leader may very well have succeeded in forging order out of chaos. At least for the time being.

Hornigold had been right about our chances of taking on more hands in Nassau. There were little to be had. Everybody was already attached to a crew and was only stopping off in Nassau for some item of business of other. We managed to take on a couple of men but eventually came to realise that the *Azrael* would be putting out to sea undermanned.

We didn't let that dampen our spirits, however. We might be short on numbers and low on powder and supplies (for we had little money to purchase either) but, for the first time, we were setting out as pirates, not fleeing into the unknown to save our skins. This time we were weighing anchor with a purpose and that purpose was to take a prize that would put us on an equal footing with the other members of the Flying Gang.

Caution was the word, however. I was under no illusions as to our vulnerability. Keen though we were, we couldn't just fall upon the first ship we sighted. Each and every potential target had to be assessed closely first. How many guns did they have? How trim were they? My crew might be made up of experienced seamen and good fighters at that, but they had not yet proven that they could work together. Even a small crew might outmanoeuvre us and bring its guns to bear before we could fire ours.

All this made finding a suitable target extremely difficult. We spent the rest of spring sailing up and down the Windward Passage and to the Straits of Florida and back, inspecting every vessel from a distance, hoping to encounter one small and weak enough. If anything, the crew got plenty of experience in sailing the *Azrael* and I put them through some training exercises to sharpen them up and get them working as a team, in particular the gun crews who I put under the command of Rogers who had been master gunner under Avery. I would have had them firing at floating targets but the small amount of powder we had in our stores was like gold dust and could not be wasted.

As the months passed our enthusiasm waned and the feeling of disappointment grew. Some pirates we were turning out to be! Every vessel that passed seemed too risky and I began to feel that the crew were starting to think I was too craven to attack anything. I am far from craven, but I am also cautious and I refused to waste men's lives by giving in to impatience. All the same, we could hardly return to Hornigold with an empty hold, and I knew that if I did not lead my crew to some sort of success that season, then my tenure as captain would be a short one.

We were able to replenish our food stores by putting in at uninhabited islands and cays for meat, fish, fruit and occasionally fresh water wherever we found a spring. Some of the older hands knew many of these spots and it was at one of them that we ran into our newest spot of trouble or perhaps our first real opportunity, depending on how you look at it.

We anchored on an island the Spanish call Vieques but is known to the British as Crab Island, about eight miles off the southeast coast of Puerto Rico. It is a popular haunt for pirates and there was something of a community there, off and on, depending on the season. In late April it was practically deserted. With little trading to be had in the settlement of tents and lean-tos (and little in our hold to trade in any case), we occupied ourselves by anchoring in a small bay on the western side of the island and began hunting wild pigs to roast.

It was when one of the hunting parties didn't return that we knew something was up.

"Damn fools have probably got lost," said Walters.

We were sitting around one of the fires watching a pig, the first party had shot, slowly turning on its spit. Thomas Moon, the ship's cook, was basting it with lime juice which drizzled over the crackling skin, running down with the fat and sizzling as it dripped onto the burning embers. Our mouths watered at our imminent meal, and I was irritated by the tardiness of the second group. We'd tuck in once the pig was done whether they had returned or not, but I couldn't dismiss the uneasy feeling that something was wrong. Harrison was in the second party and was not only our helmsman but a man I had grown to like. The feeling that something had happened to him and the others threatened to spoil my meal.

"I'm going to go and look for them," I said with a finality that surprised even myself. "Who's with me?"

The rest of the crew looked at me uneasily, each of them with half an eye on the nearly done pig. It's a hard thing to ask a meat-starved man to leave a good meal even if it's to look for lost shipmates.

"Well, I suppose I'd better come with you or I'd never hear the end of it from the crew," said Walters. "I am quartermaster, after all."

"Aye, count me in," said Rogers, casting a longing glance at the pig. "But those buggers had better have a good excuse for keeping me from my dinner."

In all, we formed a party of five and we set out with loaded pistols and sharpened blades in search of Harrison and the others leaving threats to those who remained that there had better be some roasted pork left for us or there would be dire consequences.

I led the party with a blazing brand to light our way through the jungle. The moon was nearly full but the leaves of the towering trees above us kept us in a deep gloom. We hacked through the undergrowth with our swords and called out the names of Harrison and the others.

"Where the bloody hell could they have got to?" Walters seethed. "This island is squealing with pigs. Why go so far to find one?"

"You don't suppose they've headed to the settlement on the other side, do you?" Rogers asked. "Deserted us and thrown in their lot with some other crew?"

"Belay that talk!" Walters snapped. "Harrison isn't a turncoat, even if some of the others are griping sods."

Rogers admitted as much but his words had placed a seed of doubt in my mind, though I did not voice it. The crew were unhappy. It had been a miserable season and I was failing them as their captain. Perhaps some of them had jumped ship, Harrison included. Worse yet, they might be plotting with some other crew to take the *Azrael*. I gritted my teeth and tried to find some of Walters' positivity within me but it wasn't easy with the darkness of the jungle pressing in on us and no sign of our shipmates.

"What was that?" Rogers hissed.

"What was what?" asked Walters.

"Didn't you hear it? A twig snapping behind us. We're being followed!"

"Just some animal," said Walters. "I told you this island is teeming with pigs, though why Harrison and the others couldn't find one is beyond me."

"Because Harrison and the others became prey themselves," I said slowly, drawing the party to a halt.

"What?" said Walters. "What's your meaning, Captain?"

"My meaning is that we've just walked into the same trap that Harrison's party did. We're surrounded."

I turned slowly, holding my torch at arm's length to illuminate the undergrowth around us. The others let out terrified gasps as they saw the white eyes set in dark faces that peered at us from the jungle. The torchlight glinted off pistols and rifles that were aimed at us on all sides and I recognised those firearms as belonging to Harrison and the others.

"Maroons, by God!" Walters hissed.

I had heard of maroons; escaped slaves who fled the plantations and formed isolated communities in the jungled hills. Sometimes they raided the plantations to free more slaves and strike terror into the hearts of the white planters.

"Throw down your weapons," said a deep voice.

I looked around and tried to seek out its owner but it was impossible.

"I said throw them down!"

"What assurance can you give us that you will not kill us if we do?" I said.

"We have no interest in killing you," the voice replied. "We did not kill your comrades after they had thrown down theirs."

I felt a rush of relief despite our situation. Harrison and the others were alive at least. "Where are they?" I demanded.

"Safe, for the time being. As will you be. We only wish to talk."

"Talk? You have a funny method of conversation."

"Nevertheless, you have no choice. Not if you want to live and see your friends again."

He was right. We had no idea how many of them there were and, if what their leader said was true, the lives of Harrison and the others relied on our compliance.

"Throw them down, lads," I said to my men.

"Captain?" Walters murmured.

"Do as I say!"

I led by example and set my blade down before drawing the twin pistols from my belt and laying them on the ground. My crew reluctantly did the same and two black men hurried forward to gather our weapons.

Now that we were unarmed, the leader of the maroons felt safe enough to step out from his hiding place and reveal himself. He was a large man, barefooted and clothed only in wide linen culottes. He folded his arms across his broad chest and looked me up and down.

"What is your name?" he asked me.

"I am Captain Philip Rake of the *Azrael*," I said. "This is my quartermaster, Walters. Now, as we are playing at being civil, might I have your own name?"

"I am Adolpho," the man replied.

"And you are the leader of this ... *group*?"

"We have no leader. We are free men. But, for the sake of argument, I am currently their spokesman."

"What do you want from us?"

"Come with us and we will make all plain."

Again, we had no choice but to do as we were told. Adolpho turned from us and we were accompanied by the armed blacks through the jungle. Nobody talked. Our captors clearly didn't trust us and I, like the rest of my crew, wondered if we were being led to our execution.

We emerged in a clearing atop a small headland that looked out over the crashing surf. A tiny settlement of lean-tos thatched with palms ringed a campfire. I realised at a glance that the spot had been chosen so that it would not be visible from the sea.

The maroons were around twenty in number. A small group of runaways no doubt, but I wondered from where they had fled. There were no plantations on Crab Island. A small enclosure of fresh-cut branches contained Harrison and the others, watched over by a surly black man with a rifle and cutlass.

"Your friends," Adolpho said. "Safe and sound. I would offer you some rum to drink but we have little provisions here."

"You say you want to talk to us," I said. "Why then do you capture some of my men and hold them prisoner?"

Adolpho looked at me. "Consider things from our point of view. We are twenty escaped slaves. You, by the looks of you, are pirates. To pirates are we not little more than valuable cargo to be sold on like casks of rum? How could we be sure of our safety if we approached your camp, unarmed, asking to talk? Many pirate captains would simply clap us in irons and sell us off at the nearest port. We had to make you come to us, unarmed. And by capturing some of your men, we have managed just that." He grinned, evidently pleased at their success. "But, to show that there is no ill-feeling, I release your men to you now."

At a nod from Adolpho, the enclosure was opened and Harrison and the others crept out, glancing nervously at the armed men that surrounded us.

"Have you been ill-used?" I asked Harrison.

"Can't say that we have," Harrison replied. "Though we haven't had a scrap to eat nor any drink besides water."

"Apologies for the inhospitality," Adolpho said. "But we have little enough for ourselves besides what we can scavenge from this island."

"Look here," I said in irritation. "It's about time you fellows told us what it is you want. We grow tired of these games."

"Peace, Captain Rake," Adolpho said. "No more games. Only honest talk."

"Well? Talk then."

"As I said, we are runaway slaves. We deserted a plantation on Saint Thomas and stole a small boat to make our way to Puerto Rico. Perhaps you have heard the Spaniards' position on escaped slaves from territories owned by rival nations?"

"Aye, they give them their freedom, or so it is said," Walters spoke up. "An attractive lure for slaves who dare risk it and an inventive way of damaging the workforce of other nations."

"Quite so," Adolpho replied. "There is a part of San Juan called Cangrejos which is given over to free blacks who accept baptism into the Catholic church. A small price to pay for freedom."

"I'd say you boys have lost your way," said Walters.

"Through no fault of our own but the treachery of a Spaniard called Luis de Polanco," spat Adolpho and the mention of this name drew angry scowls and curses from the assembled fugitives.

"Who's he?" I asked.

"A foul traitor who would capture escaped men and sell them back into slavery! He is a *guarda costa* who prowls these waters in his vessel called *La Cuerva* but in truth he is a red-handed pirate and slaver. He picked us up off the coast of Culebra and pretended to be a friend to fugitives from Saint Thomas. He promised that he would carry us into San Juan and personally make the arrangements for our baptism and freedom. But, as soon as we were onboard, he tried to put us in irons and head back to Saint Thomas to sell us back into bondage!"

"A Spaniard returning slaves to Saint Thomas?" Walters exclaimed. "That island is still under Danish control, is it not?"

"Aye, that it is," Adolpho replied. "And that tells you all you need to know about the honour of Don Luis de Polanco. He pretends to serve the interest of the

Spanish Crown all the while he lines his pockets by selling men to other countries like a common pirate. No offence intended."

I did not comment on that. Pirates we may be, but we were no slavers, despite whatever Walters and the others had got up to under the banner of Henry Avery. I had seen the slave markets in Madagascar and had decided long ago that I wanted no part of such a vile trade.

"How did you escape a second time?" Walters asked.

"There was fight aboard *La Cuerva*," said Adolpho. "When I complained that we had a deal that he would take us to San Juan, he told me that he did not make deals with savages. We weren't too happy about that and resisted being made to go below. They drew pistols on us and we made for the side. Many were shot down before reaching the gunwale and those of us who were lucky enough to reach the water, the Spaniards used for target practice. We swam for the shore but only three of us made it. It wasn't until we were running for the trees that I realised my brother, Nicholaus, was no longer with us.

"We delved into the interior of Culebra and hid for the next few days until the sails of *La Cuerva* could no longer be seen. Then we went down to the shore and buried our dead comrades who had washed ashore. My brother was not with them and I can only assume that he was taken back to Saint Thomas."

Adolpho's face burned with rage and shame at his inability to save his brother. "Myself, Benjamin and Francis here found a small maroon community on Culebra made up of those who do not wish to try their luck in San Juan. There we met several other fugitives from the Ensomhed plantation from which we fled, and still have family members there who suffer in bondage. We banded together and made our plans to return to Saint Thomas to rescue our brothers and sisters, to take them to freedom. But to do that, we need a ship. With guns."

"So you came here, to Crab Island," I said.

He nodded. "We knew that we would have to take our chances with the pirates in order to have a chance at rescuing our fellows."

Walters snorted at this. "What makes you think we'd help you? Or was your plan to take our ship from us? If so, you've a hard fight ahead of you for you've no weapons but those you stole from us while two-score armed men guard our vessel."

Adolpho smiled. "You mistake us, Mr. Walters. Our intentions are to bargain with you, not fight you."

"Bargain?"

"Aye. What pirates turn down the opportunity to add a ship to their fleet?"

"What ship?" I asked, my interest suddenly piqued by his words.

"*La Cuerva* was spotted off the coast of Culebra headed for Saint Thomas not two days ago. De Polanco is no doubt taking more captured fugitives to sell to Johannes Abramson, the owner of the Ensomhed plantation. That is the ship I offer to you in payment for getting me to Saint Thomas and for taking me and my people to freedom."

"Payment?" Walters chuckled. "How exactly do you plan to pay us with something that is not yours to give away?"

"*La Cuerva* will be anchored in Ensomhed Bay," Adolpho explained. "The very name means 'lonely headland' in Danish. It is an isolated spot and there are no fortifications. De Polanco will be vulnerable to attack. Once we have the ship, it will be the work of moments to lay siege to the plantation and free my brothers and sisters."

"Raiding a plantation isn't exactly in our line of work," I said, alarmed by how quickly the conversation had turned to planning an all-out attack on an unknown target. "How many guns does this *La Cuerva* have?"

"Around twenty. Perhaps twenty-four."

"That's a hell of a battle you're talking about. We would lose many men. It would be far better to use stealth rather than a blunt attack. Approach this Spaniard as friends and then, when the time is right ..."

"Captain!" Walters put in. "You're not seriously considering doing what this madman says?"

"I am merely theorising," I said. "The prospect of capturing a Spanish privateer is enticing, is it not?"

"Aye, if we can trust a word of what this black scoundrel says. And we need a better-laid plan if you are to convince the crew that this is not sheer lunacy."

"True, the plan must be worked out in detail before we commit to anything," I admitted.

Walters glared at Adolpho. "Charlotte Amalie has some of the largest slave auctions in the West Indies," he said, referring to Saint Thomas's capital on the southern side of the island. "How do you know de Polanco will sell your people back to the Ensomhed plantation in particular?"

"Because he boasted as much once we were taken onboard *La Cuerva*," Adolpho said. "In his eagerness to flaunt our fate before us, he revealed his hand. White men's arrogance is often their downfall." He grinned at Walters.

"He must have a private agreement with Abramson," I said. "No doubt he will want to keep his dealings hidden from the Spanish Crown."

"Quite so," Adolpho said. "You see, Captain Rake, it might not be as dangerous as your quartermaster fears. What say you?"

"I say you and your men accompany us to our camp where we can discuss things at length. My crew are undoubtedly concerned for my safety and my empty belly is pining for my dinner which is surely burnt to ashes by now."

Adolpho and his men were wary of a trap but seemed to know that there was no other way forward. If they wanted the use of the *Azrael* and its crew, then they would have to allow us to be their hosts.

They gave us our weapons back and, after we all assured each other that there were no hard feelings, we headed back through the jungle towards our camp. The remainder of my crew jumped up in alarm at our approach and there was a tense moment as weapons were seized. When it became known that we were not prisoners of the black men, we were able to defuse the situation.

"Where is the pork and rum?" Walters demanded. "We're famished and in sore need of a drink. Devil take the lot of you if there's none left!"

But there was still some rum and our shipmates had saved us some of the roasted pork. We shared the meagre supply with Adolpho and his men who seemed a little put out that there was not more of a bountiful feast to be had. I think they began to suspect that we were not so well-equipped a pirate crew as they had hoped for.

I explained the situation to the rest of the crew and there were audible misgivings about trusting our new companions. There is little love lost between black and white in that part of the world and many of my men feared reprisals for their past deeds, deeds which were better left unsaid in the present company.

"How many guns does your ship have?" Adolpho asked, swigging from a rum bottle as he gazed out at the *Azrael*.

"Twenty," I replied.

"Enough to rival *La Cuerva* then. But you have so few men?" He looked around at my crew, evidently disappointed that I did not command a hundred or so rogues.

"We lost many hands in Madagascar," I replied, "and have been unable to take on any more due to the season."

The fugitives seemed disheartened at this and there was much murmured discussion. I gazed at them as they talked. Many of them bore the mark of the lash and several had burn scars on their arms courtesy of the boiling pots of the sugar plantations. These were hardened men, beaten and brutalised into desperation. They weren't fighting for coin but for their freedom and the freedom of their companions. I had no doubt that they would be all the more fearsome in battle for it. Should our attack fail, the punishment for these men would be horrific and they knew it. They would rather die than be recaptured.

"My comrades fear that you do not have enough men to take *La Cuerva*," Adolpho told me. "You barely have enough to deliver her a full broadside."

"We barely have enough shot and powder for a full broadside in any case," I said. His face showed some alarm. "But you forget my words earlier, Adolpho. If we are to take *La Cuerva* and free your comrades, then we must use cunning, not brute force."

"Captain," said Walters, approaching me. "The crew would like a word. In private."

I left our new companions to their meat and drink and followed Walters down to the shore where a fo'c'sle council had been in progress. Several surly faces glared at me by the light of the campfire.

"Some of the crew aren't too happy about working with the maroons," said Walters.

"You've got that right!" said Thomas Moon the cook. "We don't even see why we should share our victuals with them much less let them onboard our ship and risk our necks on some mad errand on their behalf!"

Several of the others voiced their agreement.

"I understand your concerns," I told them. "But do you realise what we might be passing up if we refuse? A twenty-four-gun Spanish privateer waits for us at Saint Thomas! No doubt it will be loaded with stores and perhaps even the takings of their latest prize. Not to mention the fruits of the plantation which will also be ours for the taking once our black friends have liberated their people. Storehouses loaded with sugar and a fine house to loot!"

"Aye, you may dangle treats before us," said Moon, "but we are no mangy street curs to be fooled! How are we to take the ship and the plantation with a handful of men and little firepower? That's assuming we even get to our destination without having our throats cut in our sleep! To trust twenty unchained blacks aboard is madness!"

"These men could have murdered Harrison and the others but they didn't," I said. "This leader of theirs – Adolpho – is no brainless savage. He has a keen mind and his thirst for vengeance is hot. I don't believe they would do us ill while we help them achieve their goal. But you are right about our limited chances of taking the Spaniard and the plantation by force. As I explained to Adolpho, we must use our wits to trick our way into the confidence of this Luis de Polanco. I have a mind to pose as fellow privateers looking to trade with the Ensomhed plantation."

"Trade what?" Moon asked. "Our hold is as empty as our bellies."

"The details will have to be worked out but trust me when I say that I will not risk our lives in some reckless gamble. We will have a well-thought-out plan before we reach Saint Thomas."

That seemed to appease most of the crew although Thomas Moon was far from convinced. I would have to keep my eye on that one. Moon was one of Tomkinson's old crew and, like any sea cook who retains his position for long, was in good standing with the men. Such a man could sway a crew's vote should it come to it.

The following day we took on water and as much fresh fruit and meat as we could forage. Time was short if we were to catch *La Cuerva* before she put out again. Adolpho and his men were given berths in the hold and the rest of the crew steered clear of them. Distrust ran both ways and there was much silent scowling as we skirted Culebra and made our way north-east towards Saint Thomas. Moon in particular made his opinions of our passengers well known and I began to worry that he was souring the minds of more and more of the crew.

For my own part, I got to know Adolpho a little and grew to like him; surly and given to dark rages though he was. But I could hardly fault him for his moods, given all that he had been through. He told me that he had once been a warrior of the Fanti people of the Gold Coast. He and his brother were young men of great standing among their people until they had been captured and sold to the Danish West Indian Company. They had passed through the hands of several Danish masters where Adolpho had learned Danish and English before they were put to work in the cane fields of Ensomhed.

"Adolpho doesn't strike me as a particularly African name," I commented.

"It isn't," he replied. "My true name would be strange to your ears and you would not be able to pronounce it. My Danish masters gave me the name Adolpho but my people know my true name. It is a name for them to use and nobody else."

"Fair enough," I said. "Adolpho it is."

The Ensomhed plantation is on the northern side of Saint Thomas at a point where the island narrows in the middle, directly north of the capital of Charlotte Amalie. As Walters, Adolpho and I studied a chart in my cabin while the *Azrael* crept around the island's western point, we realised that the Danish militia would be quick to respond to any attack on the plantation.

"Another reason that we must utilise stealth," I said. "There's no way we can launch an attack or the whole island will be roused against us."

"What do you have in mind?" Walters asked me. "Moon was right when he said that we cannot pose as traders for we have nothing to trade."

"Then I suggest we pose as interlopers," I replied.

Both men looked at me in surprise.

"Unlicensed slavers?" Walters asked. "But we have no slaves ..." he paused as understanding dawned. "You're not thinking ..."

Adolpho growled, a dangerous fury in his eyes. "You must be out of your mind if you think that I'll allow you to sell us back to Abramson, even if it is a ruse," he said. No doubt he suspected me of a similar treachery to what de Polanco had pulled on him.

"Listen to me," I said, knowing that I was on thin ice with him and would have to work hard to retain his trust. "We have no hope of freeing your people by storming the plantation from without. Only a successful rebellion from within has any chance of success. If we could 'sell' your men back to the plantation, we would be able to sneak in nearly a score of agitators right under Abramson's nose."

"But these 'agitators' would be slaves again," Adolpho insisted. "What use would that serve?"

"If we retain you and your most trusted lieutenants, then you could sneak ashore at night with a boatload of weapons. You could distribute the arms to your men within and take the plantation in the night! The Danes won't know what's hit them."

"And what will you be doing?"

"I will be talking my way into the confidence of Luis de Polanco while my men silently capture his ship without a shot being fired. Once you have the plantation, we can start ferrying your people and whatever stores we can loot aboard and be away by dawn without the rest of the island being any the wiser!"

Adolpho was silent as he looked at me, unsure but at least considering my plan.

"It's a bold move, Captain," said Walters. "We have few men to take the Spanish vessel."

"I'm guessing most of the Spaniards will be ashore enjoying whatever entertainments Abramson offers as their host," I replied. "There will be little more than an anchor watch. Besides, if I can get myself invited to an audience ashore then there will be no reason for them to suspect anything."

"It's still risky," Walters said. "If this slave revolt fails or if anybody slips out of the plantation and warns the rest of the island, we'll have the militia down on us. We might easily sail away but these fellows run the risk of being recaptured or shot down."

"Thank you for your concern for our welfare, Walters," said Adolpho. "But we can take care of things on land. We will create a perimeter and herd the whites into the plantation house. Nobody will slip by us. You just make sure you are ready to leave on the dawn tide."

"Then you agree with my plan?" I asked.

He shrugged his massive shoulders. "I see few alternatives. This plan is dangerous but it can work."

"Then we are agreed," I said. "Walters, go and ready the crew. It is time we made our entrance and hope that the Spaniard doesn't open fire on us at first sight."

"Aye, Captain," said Walters and he left the cabin.

I turned to Adolpho. "You place a great deal of trust in a white pirate when you have been so abused by members of my race previously," I said. "Thank you."

"I trust in white man's greed," Adolpho replied with a smile. "You want that Spanish ship with its stores, powder and guns. You need our help to get it. And you trusted us not to 'murder you all in your beds' as Mr. Moon put it, because you know we need your help in freeing our fellows. You see, Captain Rake? We are as two flags united in a common goal and so we must trust each other. Is this not the way of your European nations?"

"Yes, it is," I admitted. "When they are not at war."

"It is well for you, Captain, that we are not at war."

I did not disagree with him. But I did wonder what would happen to our alliance once our 'common goal' had been achieved and who might be the first to break it.

We rounded the headland and spotted *La Cuerva* at anchor in Ensomhed Bay. The place was rightly named. Beside the plantation up in the hills, the bay was a deserted strip of white sand beneath green jungle. *La Cuerva* was the only vessel in the bay besides ours.

We took a longboat ashore; myself, Walters and a few others, with the intention of introducing ourselves to Herr Abramson. We were met by several armed men in straw hats who spoke to us in Danish. Receiving no sensible reply, one of them tried Spanish and then French.

"English?" I offered.

This brought smiles of understanding and we were able to make our business understood. The lead man spoke quite good English, albeit heavily accented. At the mention of slaves for sale an invitation was extended for an audience with Herr Abramson. We were led through the plantation and up to the big, white house that straddled the hill overlooking the cane fields and their sweating labourers.

Upon the gallery that surrounded the house, two men sat in cane chairs, a well-dressed slave standing nearby at their beck and call. One of the men was elderly with a grey wig while the other was about my age and dressed in fine silk and Spanish leather. He had the look of the sea about him and that of a profitable career. I do not mind admitting that I envied his style. Upon our introduction we learned that these men were Johannes Abramson and Luis de Polanco.

"And you wish to sell me your slaves?" Abramson said, once the pretence of pleasantries had been carried out.

"If they are to your liking, Herr," I said. "I do not have as many as I set out with from the Gold Coast for we were struck by disease and I lost many of my crew as well as over half my cargo. A mere seventeen negro bucks are all I have to sell."

"Don Luis here has recently recovered some of my runaways," said Abramson, "but not all of them. I have need of a few hands but seventeen? That is more than I need."

"Perhaps you might sell them on at Charlotte Amalie?" I suggested. "I would myself but ..."

"But you do not have a licence to do so," Don Luis said with a smile. Hs English was good, better than I had anticipated. "You are an interloper. That is why you come to the back door of a plantation hoping to sell off your diseased stock."

"My stock is healthy, I assure you, Don Luis," I said. "As are my crew. It has been many days since a man has died aboard my ship. The fever is gone and has spared the rest of us."

"I am sure Don Luis meant no offence," said Abramson. "You two are perhaps rivals in the same business and he might feel a little threatened by your presence. Especially as he so recently suffered the misfortune of having some slaves escape from under his nose, eh, Don Luis?"

The Spaniard scowled at this and sipped his rum.

"Myself, I welcome you and your business, Captain Rake," Abramson went on.

I did not doubt it. Two rival interlopers selling black market goods at the same door meant competitive prices. Herr Abramson could see this and, by the sour look on his face, so did Don Luis.

"I would be glad to take a look at your stock," said Abramson. "Although, as I said, I require only a few extra slaves for my own plantation. I might be able to take the rest of them off your hands, if the price and quality are both pleasing to me."

"Very well, Herr," I said. "I would be happy to bring them ashore to spare you a trip out to my ship."

"Much appreciated, Captain Rake."

We talked some more and I was acutely aware of Don Luis regarding me with a critical eye. He contributed little to the conversation despite his firm grasp of the language and I knew that I had caught the curiosity of a dangerous and wily man.

It was late afternoon by the time I had returned to the *Azrael* and started to ferry the seventeen black men ashore. Adolpho remained aboard along with Benjamin and Francis; his fellow escapees from Ensomhed. Their faces would no doubt be recognised if we tried to sell them back to Abramsom and so they would be the ones to sneak ashore later that night.

As I lined the seventeen men up on the beach, their hands tied, I felt sick and not just with worry that our plan might not work. Slavery turned my stomach and now I was selling men like chattel. Although it was all a pretence, it felt wretched to have anything to do with the whole business.

Abramson came down from his plantation house to take a look at them and so too did Don Luis. Adolpho's men played their parts well, though I knew it must have pained them to do it. They stood with their heads bowed as Abramson and Don Luis walked up and down the line, inspecting muscle and posture, demanding that they show their teeth to determine their health.

"How is it that your slaves are so well-fed?" Don Luis asked me. "I know how slaves who have crossed the Atlantic look, and these are in remarkable shape."

"As I said, Don Luis," I replied. "We lost many on our journey to disease. We had plenty of stores to go around and I saw no reason to lose more of my cargo by keeping up the starvation rations slaves are usually afforded. I fed them well and they survived perhaps because of it."

Don Luis gave me a smile of understanding but said nothing.

"These are quite fine specimens, I must admit," said Abramson. "I would certainly be happy to take on the three best ones for myself and I am sure I can fetch a good price for the others in Charlotte Amalie. Now remains the matter of price. But I never haggle on my feet. I invite you and your quartermaster to join me for dinner up at the house and we can work out the details."

"Thank you for you offer, Herr Abramson," I replied. "We gladly accept. May I suggest that you take the slaves now to save me the bother of ferrying them back to my ship? The haggling is, after all, a formality. I'm sure we can agree on a price."

I was careful not to appear too keen to hand the men over to him but the success of our plan rested on getting them into the plantation.

"That's very good of you, Captain," Abramson said. He turned to one of his armed attendants and gave orders in Danish for the slaves to be taken up to the plantation and found quarters.

I watched them being led away and silently swore a vow to myself that, whatever happened, I would not leave those men to their fate on this island. I had potentially handed them over to lifetimes of servitude and to do anything less would be to make me no better than the worst slavers of the Gold Coast.

I returned to the *Azrael* to prepare for dinner and, to prepare the next stage of our plan.

"Your men are inside the plantation," I told Adolpho. "You informed them to prepare every slave they can for escape tonight?"

"Aye," Adolpho said "My name is known at Ensomhed. When they hear that I am coming for them, my men will have every slave on that plantation ready to bear arms and fight for their freedom."

"Good. Now, I must go and sup with these animals. Are you and your companions ready?"

Adolpho nodded. He, Benjamin and Francis had wrapped a parcel of guns, powder, shot and cutlasses in oilskins and strapped it to a small float made from empty barrels. They would push this makeshift raft ashore under cover of night and sneak the weapons into the plantation while I made pleasant talk with Abramson.

"Good luck, Adolpho," I said. "Remember, don't let a single one of those Danish bastards escape to warn the rest of the island or we'll have a full-scale battle on our hands."

"Just make sure *La Cuerva* is in your hands before all hell breaks loose," he replied. "If those Spaniards still have their ship, then they can prevent us from escaping."

"You don't have to tell me that," I said.

He and his friends went below to get some rest before their midnight mission while I went and spoke with my crew on the matter of taking *La Cuerva*.

"It is as I suspected," I explained. "The captain and his crew are ashore so you can expect little more than an anchor watch. Even so, don't get careless. We need that ship in our hands before Adolpho and his boys unleash merry hell on land. Wait until they've gone ashore before taking the remaining longboat. Keep out of sight and make for the stern."

"What shall we do with the crew, Captain?" Harrison asked.

"Put them below," I said. "We can drop them off on some island once we have left Saint Thomas."

I left them to the sharpening of blades and loading of pistols and went into my cabin to dress for dinner. Captain Tomkinson had left me a collection of coats, shirts and breeches that were of fine stuff but altogether too large in the middle for my build. I did my best with wide belts and sashes to reel in some of the extra material but I still looked like a luffing sail on a calm day. It would have to do. I livened up the ensemble with some gold finery and a felt hat with a large red feather in it.

I drew some stifled grins as I exited the cabin in my finery and promised myself that once I had the cash and a decent port in which to spend it, I would deck myself out in finery that fit me and was becoming of a pirate captain. Let them laugh then.

Despite the need to have every hand available for the taking of *La Cuerva*, it would not do for a captain and his quartermaster to row themselves ashore so I took the luxury of having one of the men ferry us over.

It was late afternoon as we walked up the path that led to the plantation house. We were received by Abramson and introduced to his wife and two daughters. The three of them were exceedingly pretty, blonde and fair-skinned as is the Scandinavian way and it struck me then that I might be playing a part in seeing these three lovely ladies torn down from their perch and ground into the mud. Perhaps raped. Perhaps murdered. It all depended on how far Adolpho's vengeance extended and, despite the disgust I held for their patriarch, I hoped it would not extend to women and children. The truth was that I didn't really know. I had no idea of what I had unleashed on these people.

We drank port in the salon as Abramson boasted to us of his plantation and its profits. Don Luis was there, dressed in his Spanish foppery and he wore the bored expression of a man who had already weathered Abramson's hot air more than once. I knew that the matter of the slaves would not be broached at least until we sat down for dinner. It was still early evening and I wanted to draw out the negotiations for as long as possible in order to give Adolpho enough time to execute his takeover of the plantation. When the fighting started, things would get pretty hot in here. Walters and I would have to play dumb until the slaves marched on the house and we could take Abramson and Don Luis hostage. By then, my crew should have taken *La Cuerva* and we could begin looting the plantation and ferrying the freed slaves to the ships.

I had already decided to make Walters captain of *La Cuerva*. It would pain me to have to appoint a new quartermaster for the *Azrael* and I would miss his guidance, but I needed an experienced man to captain our new vessel and I trusted no other not to take her from me.

We soon found ourselves sitting down to a fine meal with our glasses filled with French wine by white servants. It surprised me that a man like Abramson did not use his slaves for I had heard of many wealthy whites training blacks in all manner of household work. By way of conversation, I brought this up with Abramson.

"It has become more and more the custom on this island and others for planters to fill their houses with Negroes but I insist on keeping them in the fields. The population of Saint Thomas is over seventy percent African and should they take it into their savage minds to attack the white population, they could snuff us out like a candle. These boys who pour your wine are indentured servants. Criminals from Europe sent to the Caribbean to work off their sentences alongside the Negroes. Thieves, murderers and traitors they may be, I would much prefer their presence in my house and around my family to the Negroes. We whites must stick together against such odds. This is not a point that many other planters consider."

I saw the logic in Abramson's caution. I did not know how savagely he dealt with his slaves but they were his slaves nonetheless and men like Adolpho despised their position enough to risk their lives in trying to escape. I did not doubt that Abramson's fears for his safety were well-grounded, much good it might do him tonight.

I glanced at the surly but silent faces of the men who served us. One was elderly and grizzled while the other was little more than a boy, both with nothing but years of servitude ahead of them at the beck and call of a villain like Abramson. I had heard of England's criminals being sent to its colonies to live out their lives as little more than slaves. I myself had been indentured to an East Indiaman rather than rot in prison and I would be aboard it still had I not taken my fortune into my own hands.

I saw that Walters was also regarding the servants with quiet consideration. No doubt he was thinking of his own life which, had things worked out otherwise, may have turned a similar path. As the old man and the youth headed back to the kitchen house, I thought grimly, *there, but for the grace of God, walk Walters and me.*

As our meal came to its conclusion, I looked out the slatted jalousie windows at the fields of sugar cane. Night had fallen and the warm evening breeze drifted in, making the candles flicker, threatening to snuff them out. I wondered if Adolpho and his men had made it to the shore yet. The silence of the grounds beyond the house spoke of all going to plan. I had no doubt that the slightest misstep would be signalled to us with the firing of shots and the ringing of bells.

"Now," said Abramson. "I fear we must turn to the sordid talk of business. Ladies, I wonder if you would excuse us? I would hate to bore you."

Fru Abramson and the two blonde daughters rose from their seats and, with polite smiles and bowing heads, they left the dining room, leaving only myself, Walters, Abramson and Don Luis at the table. Abramson called for brandy and we settled in for the negotiation process.

"You have some very impressive specimens, Captain Rake," he said, swirling his brandy around in his glass. "It is only a shame that so few made it across the Atlantic."

"Disease aboard a ship is a terrible thing, Herr Abramson," I replied, taking a deep gulp of my brandy. "We were lucky to survive at all."

"Quite so," said Don Luis. "And your stock in such remarkable condition too. I took a closer look at them while you were aboard your ship. I could not resist. I am something of a connoisseur when it comes to working Negroes. You say you purchased these fellows on the Gold Coast?"

"That I did, Don Luis," I replied.

"Then how is it, Captain Rake, that one of them bears the mark of Don Alfaro, an acquaintance of mine who has a plantation on the southern coast of Puerto Rico?"

I was silent, not sure how to play this. These owner's 'marks' were little more than initials branded

152

into the flesh, warped by time and scarring. I could deny that the mark was that of his fellow Spaniard but then, there was no denying that the slave carried a mark of some sort. If I truly was an interloper who had purchased slaves on the Gold Coast, then they would be new, unmarked slaves. I cursed myself for not checking them and keeping any who had such marks aboard with Adolpho.

Don Luis took my hesitation as a sign of his triumph. "Herr Abramson, these men are playing you false!" he cried. "They are not honest slavers but pirates trying to sell you somebody else's stock!"

"That wouldn't be petty jealousy talking now would it, Don Luis?" I asked, trying to appear calm. I could detect Walters tensing beside me. It was going to take some smart talking to get out of this spot. "I assure you, I have no intention of rivalling you as Herr Abramson's main dealer."

"Jealousy?" Don Luis sneered. "Of a common sea dog like you? I have hanged men far greater than you from their own yardarms. As God is my witness, I will see you hang too, high above the harbour of *La Habana* for an English pirate!"

"In order to take me to *La Habana*," I said coolly, "you will need a ship. And I do believe that if you signal to your ship out in the bay, you will receive the message that she is in the hands of my men and your own brave souls are below in irons."

It was a cocky bit of talk for I had no idea if my men had succeeded in taking *La Cuerva* yet, but I had no cards left to play. Don Luis had rumbled me and all I could do was put on a brave face and hope things would work out in my favour.

But, by the sickening grin on the Spaniard's face, things were decidedly *not* working out in my favour.

"I am afraid you are overly presumptive, Rake," he said. "You see, once I realised that your talk of coming from the Gold Coast was a lie, I grew suspicious as to your intentions here. So much so, that I sent a detachment of my men out to your ship while we dined. Whatever you had hoped to achieve, I can assure you that if *you* look out over the bay, you will see the cross of Borgoña currently flying from your ship."

I gritted my teeth, willing his talk to be all lies. Had I really been so utterly outmanoeuvred? But Don Luis seemed to be ignorant of Adolpho and the other fugitives from Ensomhed. That meant that they had probably made it to the shore and into the plantation before Don Luis's men had set out across the bay. All chances for our success now rested on Adolpho taking over the plantation. If we could get Don Luis and Abramson into our custody, we might bargain our way out of this mess.

There was a gunshot somewhere out in the darkness. Don Luis leapt to his feet. Abramson would have too had he been a younger man, but alarm showed in his face, nonetheless. I allowed myself a small grin. This was something unanticipated for the Spaniard.

"What's going on out there?" Don Luis snapped at Abramson.

"I don't know," the Dane replied. "Could be that some fool accidently fired his pistol. I will have some of my men investigate it at once."

I said nothing, happy to let Abramson's guards fall unwittingly into whatever Adolpho and his boys were stirring up on the plantation.

More gunshots cracked out and we moved over to the windows. The lights of burning structures could be seen in the velvety-green darkness like beacons.

"It's a slave revolt!" Abramson cried. "Hanne! Elisabet! Margrete!"

His wife and daughters emerged from the salon, their faces pale and frightened. Abramson ordered them upstairs and then demanded one of his servants fetch his pistols. The old coot was preparing to defend his home and family personally. He ordered his men to bolt all the doors then take position in the upstairs windows.

While all this chaos was unfolding, Don Luis had not taken his eyes off Walters and me. He had evidently gathered from my amused expression that we had played some part in this. He drew his pistol and pointed it at my head.

"What are you doing, Don Luis?" Abramson demanded. "Save your powder! We might have every Negro on the plantation upon us at any minute!"

"This English dog is at the root of this!" the Spaniard declared. "How convenient that the day you purchase slaves from him, the entire plantation revolts."

Abramson glared at me. "Did you plant insurrectionists in my plantation?"

I smiled at him. "I merely returned some of your slaves to you."

Abramson frowned, not quite taking my meaning, but I didn't care. He would understand soon enough when Adolpho broke down his door. But Walters and I would have to help him somehow.

Unarmed as we were, I started to look around for any opportunity to overcome Don Luis and Abramson so that we might seize their pistols and take them hostage. Don Luis seemed wise to my plan for he dealt me a blow to the gut with his left fist that doubled me over. Walters leapt to my defence but backed down with the Spaniard's pistol in his face. Don Luis barked orders to his men and we were seized by the arms.

"Where are you taking them?" Abramson asked.

"To my ship," Don Luis said.

"You're abandoning me?" Abramson's face was stricken with fear.

"I am not your private guard, Herr Abramson. I suggest you either leave in whatever vessel you own or barricade yourself up in this mansion and hope the island's militia will be here soon to relieve you."

"You ... you bastard!" Abramson yelled as we were hauled out of the room, his voice trembling with panic.

As we emerged into the warm night air on the house's northern side, we could hear the sound of fighting close by. The bay was below us and when I saw the *Azrael* with the Spanish flag of a blood-red cross on a white field fluttering at her stern, I knew that Don Luis had not been bluffing. I had lost my ship and my crew.

As we made our way down the path towards the beach, there were several gunshots from the trees to our left. Walters and I threw ourselves to the dirt as the Spaniards returned fire but it was like shooting at shadows. One of the Spaniards fell with a pistol ball in his face and Don Luis yelled at his men to make for the water.

We were manhandled down to the beach and bundled into a longboat. Don Luis sat at the prow as we were rowed out to *La Cuerva*, his pistol never leaving us for an instant. Clambering aboard, we were taken to the Great Cabin and stood under the watchful eye of the first mate while Don Luis gave orders for both *La Cuerva* and the *Azrael* to put out to sea.

"Those black dogs of yours have surrounded Abramson in his mansion, the poor fool," Don Luis said to us. "But they'll not live to see another sunset. By dawn the whole island will be turned against them. With no way to leave, they will be trapped and butchered."

I ground my teeth together in frustration. He was absolutely right. I had utterly failed in my oath to help those poor devils escape. I had ferried them to their doom.

Don Luis walked behind his table and placed his pistol upon it. He unstopped a decanter of brandy and poured himself a measure. Only he, his mate, Walters and I were in the cabin and I desperately looked around for some way we could take over the ship and reverse our fortunes.

"You can stop casting your villainous eyes about my cabin looking for a way to escape," Don Luis said, catching my roving eyes. "By tomorrow, my dear *capitán*, you will be in a gaol cell awaiting the pleasures of *La Habana*'s hangman."

"By tomorrow, you will be feeding the crabs at the bottom of this bay," said a voice by one of the open windows.

A figure squatted there, silhouetted against the moonlit sky and I only caught a glimpse of him before he pounced, panther-like, seizing Don Luis, the glint of a blade at his throat. It was Adolpho, dripping wet from his swim from the shore. His eyes blazed with a fury and the knife pressed deep into the soft flesh of the

Spaniard's throat, barely restrained by the hand that grasped it.

The mate raised his pistol to fire at the intruder but I, seizing my chance, barrelled into him, knocking him off balance. The gun went off and the ball thudded into the ceiling. The mate dropped the pistol and drew his knife, preparing to come at me. Walters grabbed Don Luis's pistol from the table and fired at the mate, felling him instantly.

The cabin was thick with gunpowder smoke and we could hear cries of alarm on deck. I quickly bolted the doors to the Great Cabin. We had Don Luis by the balls now and I was going to use him for all he was worth.

"By Jove, Adolpho!" Walters said as he reloaded the captain's pistol. "You're a trump card!"

"We have the plantation house surrounded," Adolpho said. "But, when I saw you and Captain Rake being led down to the beach and the Spanish flag flying from the *Azrael*, I knew I had to act fast to save all of our skins."

"Well, you might have just done it, friend," I said. "But it all depends on how much this Spanish cockerel's crew love him." I took the loaded pistol from Walters and pointed it at Don Luis's head. "Tell your crew that I want my ship back. Get every one of your Spanish dogs off the *Azrael* and lined up on deck here, unarmed and ready to be placed in irons."

"You'll never get away with this!" Don Luis spluttered, still writhing under Adolpho's knife.

"Maybe not," I admitted. "But I'm damn well going to try and if you think I'm bluffing, then we'll give you something to convince you otherwise. Adolpho, cut off one of his fingers, if you please."

Adolpho removed the knife from the Spaniard's throat and, seizing one of his hands in his massive paw, he pinned it to the tabletop. He then placed the edge of the knife against a ring-laden finger.

"No! Wait!" Don Luis squealed. "I beg you! Let me talk to my men!"

"Lively then."

The crew, who had begun to pound on the doors to get in and save their captain ceased as Don Luis called out to them in Spanish. Walters and I had no idea what he was telling them, but it didn't matter. If Don Luis wanted to save his skin, then he would do exactly as we asked.

It took some time for messages to be relayed to the *Azrael* and for the longboats to return, but return they did. As the Spaniards climbed back aboard *La Cuerva*, we could see the Spanish flag being struck and the black flag being raised by my crew as proof that the ship was now back under our control.

I had Rogers and a few other crew members from the *Azrael* come aboard and help Walters and I clap the Spaniards in irons below. We kept Don Luis on deck, close to us should any of his men decide on any heroics. His life hung by a thread and he knew it.

"Well, Captain," Walters said to me once the hatches were battened, sealing the Spaniards in the gloom. "This was a roundabout way of doing it, but we have *La Cuerva*!"

"*You* have *La Cuerva*, my friend," I told him.

"I don't take your meaning, Captain."

"I want you to captain her for me."

"Don't you need me aboard the *Azrael*?" he asked, though I could see the trace of a smile that threated to split his grizzled old mug from ear to ear.

"I'll just have to trust in Rogers and Harrison to steer me straight."

"Well, thank you, Captain! She and I will do you proud!"

The fight was still going on ashore and, by looking at the hills through my spyglass, I could see stabs of flame from the upstairs windows of the plantation house as Abramson and his men tried to fend off the slaves that had surrounded it on all sides.

"We could use Don Luis here to persuade Abramson to open his doors to us," I said, though I didn't have much faith in that approach. After Don Luis abandoned Abramson to his fate, I suspected the Dane would not care a fig what we did with our hostage.

"No," said Adolpho. "This bastard slaver and I have unfinished business." He seized Don Luis by his lapels and pointed his pistol at his face. "Now that we have our passage off this rock, I can finally take my vengeance."

"Vengeance?" Don Luis cried.

"Aye, for my brother! I learned from the others on the plantation why my brother never made it to the shores of Culebra with us. He was shot by your men as he tried to swim for freedom. He was always a slower swimmer than me and I will bear the shame that I never looked back for him. But you, Don Luis, you as good as threw him to the sharks yourself."

The muzzle of the pistol pressed against the Spaniard's lips and Adolpho forced it in between his teeth, filling his mouth with cold metal.

160

"We had a bargain!" Don Luis tried to say around the barrel of the gun.

"I don't make deals with savages," Adolpho said.

There was a brief moment of understanding and Don Luis's eyes widened as he realised that his own words were coming back to haunt him before Adolpho pulled the trigger.

The blast took the back of the Spaniard's head off and sprayed blood and brains up the deck. Adolpho let the corpse fall to the floor and turned to face us, his pistol smoking and his blood-spattered face sporting the grim look of vengeance satisfied.

"Well, so much for bargaining with Abramson," I said. "Come on, let's get into the longboat and go and give your comrades a hand."

We dumped the bodies of Don Luis and his mate over the side and lowered the longboat. I left an anchor watch to guard the prisoners and Walters rowed us ashore. As we hurried up to the house, we could hear cheers of victory and knew that something had happened.

"They're in!" Walters cried. "They have the doors down!"

Nothing but a splintered crater remained of the front doors to the mansion. The felled log with which the slaves had used to batter them down lay cast to one side. They were inside the house and we could hear the shouts and gunfire of the last ditch defence.

By the time we made our way in and upstairs, it was over. The remnants of the Danish defenders lay sprawled in pools of blood, either shot or cut down or beaten with clubs. The blacks had armed themselves with anything that came to hand. As it became known that Adolpho had returned to them, great cheers went up to hail their hero.

We were taken to the master bedroom where Abramson and his family cowered under the guns of the slaves. Abramson had been beaten nearly to a pulp and I was surprised that he was still alive. He had been kept for Adolpho's judgement, it seemed. His wife and daughters seemed to be unharmed for which I was glad, though I didn't know how long they would remain so.

"What's to be done with them?" Benjamin asked Adolpho.

Adolpho looked down on his former owner and the architect of the misery of he and his people with utter scorn. "He will pay for his crimes," he said. "With his life."

The women screamed and begged as Abramson was dragged away. There was little I could do about it and I didn't have much of a mind to interfere on the old Dane's behalf anyway. He was filth and the world was well shot of him.

They dragged him up to the highest window in the house and looped a rope around his neck before shoving him out. His neck did not break and he was left to choke and dance the hempen jig while the liberated blacks whooped and cheered.

The house was summarily ransacked of its finery, its food and its drink. The people who had toiled in its shadow for so many years, denied everything but the barest and most degrading existence, now revelled in their roles as conquerors. The kitchens yielded food of a quality and quantity they had only ever dreamt of and the wine stores were broken into with equal zeal. They danced in the rooms and halls of their late master dressed in his rich clothes and drinking his finest liquor.

I was able to plead for the safety of the women and Adolpho gave orders that they were not to be touched. They would remain here in the ruins of their former life and tell those who came for them of what had happened here. As for the coming of others from the island's interior, I was keen to start loading the ships. It would be dawn before long and I wished to be away.

It was quite a task to halt the celebrations but Adolpho managed it through a combination of the respect he commanded and his barked orders and threatened blows from his pistol butt. He got everybody into some sort of order and we went down to the storehouses to take stock.

We were not disappointed. They were stuffed with sacks of sugar and barrels of molasses awaiting shipment. There wasn't a moment to lose if we were to capitalise on this windfall so I had the Spanish prisoners removed from the hold of *La Cuerva* and chained up on the beach. We needed the room for our booty.

We worked through what was left of the night ferrying goods out to the ships. We stripped both the mansion and the storehouses of whatever we could use for ourselves or sell on at a profit. Most of the goods we stowed in *La Cuerva* and kept the *Azrael* free for transporting the passengers to their new home, wherever that might be.

Dawn was tinging the sky to the east with a pink hue by the time we were ready to weigh anchor and head out of the bay. Walters was aboard *La Cuerva* getting used to his new command while I stood with Harrison and Adolpho at the helm of the *Azrael*.

"Do you still have your hearts set on San Juan?" I asked Adolpho.

He shook his head. "I no longer trust any olive branch offered by the Spanish. No, my people and I must find our own home. Take us to Culebra. There are many maroons there who would welcome us."

He headed below to see to the quartering of his people. Thomas Moon approached me and I could see that several of the more disagreeable elements of my crew were at his back. Whatever he had to say to me apparently could not be said without support.

"Captain," he began. "We've been thinking."

"Dangerous habit," I said. "Have you made sure the galley is stocked?"

"It's them Negroes that we wanted to talk to you about."

"What about them?"

"Well, Captain. We have a hold full of them, you see. A *cargo*, you might say."

"I wouldn't."

"A precious cargo," he went on. "One we might sell at any port."

"Drop that thought, Moon," I snapped. "Those are free men."

"Well, they don't have to be," Moon said. "Me and the lads feel that we're missing out on our share if we just ... *let them go*."

"You have no share in them, Moon," I said. "They are passengers and what's more, one of them saved my life. We are taking them to Culebra as promised. Now, get about your business."

Moon's face turned sour. "What use is it in having a captain who doesn't do what's best for his crew?" he demanded. "You're letting good coin slip through our fingers and we don't like that!"

"Too bad!" I snapped. I knew I was in trouble here. If a majority of the crew felt the same way about our passengers as Moon did, then I could be voted out as captain. But I would be damned if I broke my promise to Adolpho.

I managed to get Moon and his followers back to their work, though I sorely missed Walters' presence. We set sail and headed west for Culebra.

The maroons had made their homes in the fastness of the hills which provided a good view of the beach so they were aware of our presence long before we dropped anchor in the bay. I made sure to pack the first longboat with Adolpho and as many of his men as possible. The sight of free black men bearing arms would hopefully show that we were no slavers.

Adolpho knew the way to the settlement in the hills, but we waited at the edge of the jungle for a delegation of armed maroons to come down to us. Once they realised that Adolpho and the others had returned and that we white men were friends, we were graciously welcomed. And, when it became known that we had a hold full of freed people from Saint Thomas, the attitude was ecstatic.

After ferrying everybody ashore, we were invited up to the maroon settlement where a great feast was held that night to celebrate the emancipation of the Ensomhed plantation and the deaths of both Don Luis and Gustav Abramson. We ate roasted pork, crab and fish as well as mangoes and yams which the maroons cultivated themselves. Rum was plentiful and there was singing and dancing late into the night.

I was a little the worse for wear when Adolpho approached me, slumped as I was against the wall of one of the palm-thatched houses.

"You putting out tomorrow, Captain?" he asked me.

I shrugged. "I suppose so. I don't want to draw any attention to this community by having my ships anchored in the bay for longer than necessary. People will be looking for us now; Spaniards most likely. Perhaps Abramson's people. One does not loot a plantation and free all its slaves without somebody trying to do something about it."

"I want to come with you," he said. "If you have a place in your crew for me. Benjamin and Francis wish to join you too."

"Why?" I asked, looking around at the happy community of free people. "This place is a peaceful hideaway from the world. And you are a hero to these people."

"Some may be content to live out their days here in secret. In isolation. They have everything they ever dreamed of and thought they would never get while they toiled under the lash on the plantations. But I am no farmer and I have no family. Not anymore."

"But here you would be safe. The road I take is a dangerous one."

"Let me ask you something, Captain. Would you be content to be poor but safe for the rest of your life or would you constantly crave something more?"

I considered the events of my life so far and knew how many of them were down to my own making. Had I been content to work for an honest wage and a peaceful life, I would be a cooper in Bristol now instead of a landless pirate. "I see what you mean, Adolpho," I said.

"I am a warrior," he said. "I am not made to spend my life fishing and thatching huts. I want to join you and make a fortune that no black man has ever amassed."

The combination of the rum in my belly and Adolpho's fiery words lit the fuse of passion in me and I made to stand up. Adolpho had to help me but once we were both on our feet, I clapped him on the back. "Then you shall join us, Adolpho," I said. "And Benjamin and Francis too. I would be proud to have such bully boys in my crew. We'll cut such a swathe across the Caribbean that our names will be spoken of in fear from here to London! Now, this calls for a drink. Let's find some more rum!"

Our revived celebrations were cut short as Rogers came over to me with some concerning news.

"Moon and some of the others aren't with us," he said.

"What do you mean? Where are they?" I demanded, a queasy feeling settling in my gut.

"Nobody has seen them for hours," Rogers replied. "They've been very quiet the whole evening and now ... gone."

"Fetch Walters, Harrison and Solomon," I said. "I don't like the look of this."

Myself and my most trusted men left the others to the festivities and we hurried down to the bay, armed and ready for trouble. When we got to the longboats, we found one missing and the others scuttled. Out in the bay, we could see the *Azrael* at anchor but *La Cuerva* had unfurled its sails and was steadily making its way towards the open sea.

"Those bastards!" I yelled.

"All that sugar," Rogers said.

Secretly I was glad they had taken *La Cuerva* and not the *Azrael* but it still made me enraged. I don't like being stolen from, even when I had been a stripling in the streets of Bristol but now Moon had made off with a hold full of sugar and a good portion of my crew. He was welcome to his wretched followers but I doubted the anchor watch Walters had left aboard had been part of his plan. They had now either been convinced to join Moon or they had been dispensed with.

I fetched the rest of my men from the village and we borrowed log canoes from the maroons to row out to the *Azrael* and make ready to give chase.

"*La Cuerva* is a fast ship," said Walters. "But it is weighed down with its cargo. We'll catch it."

"And I'll skin that Moon bugger and sun dry him," I vowed.

"Begging your pardon, Captain," said Walters, "but you'll have to wait your turn. That's *my* ship he's stolen."

PART 4 – THE SPANISH MAIN, SUMMER TO WINTER 1715

We gave chase but *La Cuerva* had too much of a lead on us and we lost sight of her as we entered the Turks and Caicos Islands. I seethed at our failure. Adolpho's vengeance and freed slaves aside, I felt like everything we had achieved in the season so far had been stolen from us by Thomas Moon and his confederates. I had an empty hold and no hope of filling it for we had even fewer hands aboard than when we had set out.

"We had best take a prize soon," Walters warned me. "The crew's spirits are low. We're well into the season and have nothing to show for it."

"You don't have to tell me that," I said irritably. "But we can hardly take any prizes with barely enough men to crew the ship."

We made for Nassau. There really wasn't any alternative. We asked around at the ramshackle taverns if anybody had sighted *La Cuerva* but she had not passed through the Bahamas. I knew that if we could recapture her the crew would be pleased enough but, with no leads as to where she was, it could take weeks to find her. We needed something to tide us over in the meantime.

There were more people in Nassau this time and we were able to sign on a few hands. Walters helped me come up with the articles, modelled on Avery's ones. The captain gets two shares of all prizes, quartermaster a share and a half and every crewmember one share each. With hints that we were hunting a Spanish schooner laden with sugar, we signed on nearly a full crew and set out with much higher hopes than when we had limped into Nassau.

We sailed into the Florida Straits and began hunting for prey. Not two days into it, we spotted a Spanish sloop on its way to Havana. As we closed in, I knew that this was to be the moment of truth for me. My palms were sweaty as we ran up the black flag. I am no coward in a fight but as of yet, I had never hurled myself into a sea battle in which the flash of pistols and slash of cutlasses would be all around me. I had taken to my sword lessons well but facing an enemy who had been equally or better trained than me was to be my true baptism of fire.

The sloop fired its guns at us and we retorted with a broadside that raked them from stem to stern. Their sails and rigging in tatters, we crept alongside of them admirably under Harrison's steady hands. I had the men arm themselves and those with muskets to scramble up the rigging and return fire at those on the sloop's deck who had started taking pot shots at us. We felled a couple of them, and they quickly struck their colours.

The Spanish captain was in a rage but he refrained from putting his crew into danger by doing anything about it. I was able to understand some of his grumbled insults for I had been taking lessons from Miguel, a Spaniard in my crew. With Spain rivalling England for its stake in the Caribbean, I felt that a good grasp of Spanish was as important as the ability to wield a sword.

The sloop was carrying a cargo of thirty casks of brandy which put smiles on the faces of my crew. We transferred the cargo as well as provisions and all the shot and powder they carried for we were still short on that front. We left the Spaniards with the sloop so they might carry themselves to Havana.

We sailed along the coast of Cuba and made for Jamaica where I had a mind to sell the brandy as well as see if there had been any sightings of *La Cuerva*. When we put in at Kingston, I was pleased to be surrounded by so many English voices for, although most of my crew were English, it is really quite something else to tread the boardwalks of a town that would almost feel like England were it not for the blazing sun and palm trees.

"Kingston is the centre of trade for the English," Walters said to me as we wetted our whistles in a harbourside tavern. "There'll be a higher class of buyer here. Merchants who have more *particular* tastes."

"You're talking about the stone, aren't you?" I said, refraining from referring to the Molucca Star by name in such a crowded and public place.

"Aye, that I am, Captain. We could never sell the thing in Nassau, but here ... if you know who to ask."

"I hope you know that I intend to go shares with the whole crew," I said.

"Aye, that's fair and according to articles. There'll be more than enough to make us all rich men."

"What will you do with your share?"

He sighed. "I'm old, Captain. There's not many years left in me and I want to spend some of them on land with my wife and daughter."

I widened my eyes at my quartermaster. "You have a family? You never said ..."

"I don't like to mention them, to be honest. They're perhaps the one decent thing I've done in my life and they belong to my private thoughts. I don't want them tainted by the life we live out here. I'm a bad man who's

171

done and seen too much in this world to deserve anything other than a violent death with no hope of salvation. But if there's a chance I might return to them and spend my final days being the husband and father I never was, then by God, I'll take it."

"Your cut of the stone will set them up for life," I said.

"Aye. I've been no good for them for all my adventures. I was once as rich as Croesus; we all were who sailed under Avery. But by the time we made it home, we had little left to show for it. This time I want it to be different. I want to make it up to them. My girl is married now, with babes of her own but they live poorly. I want to be able to leave them something so they know I wasn't just a useless scoundrel who was nothing but a burden to them. Anyway, what of you? Will you return home to live like a lord?"

"Home?" I said. "I don't know if that's a possibility for me. I was a criminal even before I turned pirate. Besides, I have nothing left to go back to now."

We said nothing for a while and just stared into our drinks.

"Either way, it's best we get rid of it," Walters said eventually. "Every day we stay afloat out there, we risk losing it."

"The damn thing's burning a hole through the ship," I admitted. "Its sale could mean a lot of things for a lot of us. But as you said, we could never sell it in Nassau and I don't know if I can trust any of the fences here."

"We don't take it to some common fence. We find a specialist. A merchant who deals in precious stones. Somebody with connections in London or Antwerp."

"Are we likely to find somebody like that here?"

"It's a possibility. But we'd have to play our cards close to our chest. If anybody gets wind of what we've got, then our lives won't be worth spit."

We put out feelers hoping that we might snare a diamond merchant but, as the weeks passed, we got no bites. Our search for *La Cuerva*, however, did begin to yield fruit at last. Some English sailors claimed to have seen a vessel of her description fleeing a Spanish brigantine in the Gulf of Honduras. I rounded up my crew and we set out as quickly as we were able. The Molucca Star could wait for another day, but I wasn't going to let *La Cuerva* slip away from me a second time!

It was late June and the hurricane season had already started but the weather was fine as we threaded the Cayman Islands. After briefly putting in at the Isle of Pines, we headed southwest towards the Gulf of Honduras.

Thirty miles west of the Cayman Islands we spotted a Spanish mail ship beating its way south. Mail ships had been specified by Hornigold as choice targets for they might carry correspondence to and from Havana pertaining to the treasure fleet that was due to set out any day now.

We swooped to intercept it. It tried to run, but we had the weather gauge of it and they struck their colours after a brief exchange of cannon fire. Once aboard, I interrogated the captain myself, keen to put the Spanish I had learned to use, with Miguel standing by to help out. The captain seemed to forget his fear a little, so amused he was by an Englishman speaking to him in his own tongue and we had a fair conversation despite the circumstances.

I pressed him to tell me if he had seen any vessel that matched the description of *La Cuerva* and, to our brief delight, he mentioned her by name. I had to get Miguel to translate the exact series of events but it seemed that *La Cuerva* had been prowling those waters as we had suspected but had been seized by a Spanish privateer captain by the name of Ramírez. They had put up a strong fight but were no match for the larger Spanish vessel and its experienced crew. Moon and the others, along with our cargo of sugar, had been taken to Havana and word had it, the English pirates had already been executed.

The news was devastating to our spirits. We had traipsed across the Caribbean for months in search of Moon and a reckoning, only to have it snatched from us by the Spaniards. I began to worry that my crew would mutiny there and then but fortune, however, was not such a cruel mistress as to leave us with nothing. As luck would have it, the mail ship was on its way to Cartagena and carried, along with a cargo of Madeira, some letters of import from the officials in Havana.

I put Miguel to work in reading the dispatches and he came up trumps with a letter from General Antonio de Echeverz y Subiza to his son, Manuel in Cartagena. This letter requested that his son come in person aboard the vessel known as *La Hollandesa*, with the 'queen's jewels' as quickly as possible.

"Whatever the 'queen's jewels' are, *La Hollandesa* sounds like quite a prize," I remarked.

"They are most likely the jewels personally requested by King Felipe's new strumpet," Miguel said. "He has recently remarried, and the word is that the sly wench will not consummate their marriage until she is bedecked in jewels of her own choosing from the New World."

"No wonder there is the need for such haste," I said with a grin. "Poor old King Felipe must suffer blue balls while he waits for his queen's gift to arrive from America."

"Look here, Captain," said Miguel, examining the letter further. "Echeverz states that *La Hollandesa* must arrive in Havana before the 24th of July as 'the date for departure is fixed.'"

"My god," I exclaimed. "The jewels will probably be carried to Spain with the treasure fleet. That's the date they will set out – the 24th of this month!"

"That doesn't give us much time to tell Hornigold," said Walters. "Or for him to put whatever plan he has into effect."

"The letter gives no word on which route the fleet will be taking?" I asked Miguel.

"No, Captain."

"Then we must make for Nassau with all haste," I said. "We've lost *La Cuerva* but we might make up for it tenfold if we can earn Hornigold's favour and get in on this raid! On deck now, boys! Finish up here and get the *Azrael* underway."

"The cargo of Madeira?" Walters asked.

"Leave it. We haven't the time but we do have something worth far more than a score of hogsheads!"

But when we got on deck and explained the situation to the crew, I found them less than enthusiastic to go tearing back to Hornigold with our valuable information.

"These queen's jewels, or whatever they are," spoke up an Italian called Fiaschetti, "could be ours if we stay in these waters. Why go back to Nassau now when we could wait here and grab that ship when it sets out from Cartagena?"

"One ship, even if it carries royal treasure, pales in comparison to what we might get if we join Hornigold's raid on the whole fleet," I said.

"Aye, *might*!" Fiaschetti cried. "Who's to say Hornigold will cut us in?"

"He'll need every ship he can get his hands on if he is to take one of those treasure galleons," Walters said. "They'll be heavily guarded."

"Exactly!" somebody else piped up. "We might not even get one! And if we do we'll have to go shares with a dozen other crews!"

"Shares in a galleon groaning with silver and gold dust and silks!" I protested. "We'd be rich as kings if we had to share with twenty crews!"

But my own crew remained unconvinced. They wanted *La Hollandesa* and I knew that the loss of *La Cuerva* and all we had recently gained meant that they did not have enough patience to go to Nassau and hand over our valuable information to Hornigold instead of using it for ourselves. They were men accustomed to quick gratification and did not put much trust in long term plans. Better to grab what you can in the instant than risk coming out with nothing, that was their way of thinking.

We held a vote. The Spanish crew remained under guard and watched with bemused incomprehension as this pirate crew argued with itself. In the end, it was decided that we would wait for *La Hollandesa* and forget about the treasure fleet. I sighed. There was nothing I could do about it. The crew needed a quick prize and had neither the patience nor the faith in me that was required for my plan.

We transferred the cargo of Madeira to the *Azrael* but left the dispatches. If we were to nab *La Hollandesa*, then Echeverz's letter had to reach his son in Cartagena. We let the mail ship head off and then took our time following it, heading slightly east for a small port town on the Spanish Main called Barranquilla.

Built on the swampy mouth of a river, Barranquilla is mostly occupied by Indians and traders and we were able to sell our cargo of Madeira. The crew were happy to have some coin in their purses but there wasn't much sport to be had in Barranquilla. We put out to sea not long after that, keen to cruise the route to Cuba, our eyes peeled for *La Hollandesa*.

The end of July was approaching and we knew that Don Miguel Echeverz would have to sail soon if he was to make Havana in time to join the fleet. It was on the eleventh day after we had put out from Barranquilla that Walters spotted a small ship flying Spanish colours.

"Six guns," he said, peering through my spyglass. "Dutch made, by the look of her."

"*La Hollandesa*?" I remarked, considering the meaning of the name for the first time.

"Possibly a Dutchman the Spaniards took," Walters replied.

We moved to intercept, running up Spanish colours to trick them into thinking we were their countrymen. As the distance closed, I had Miguel hail them with a concocted story of requiring a surgeon to tend to a wounded man but they refused to heave to. Further hailing resulted in no answer and I concluded that they were either in too much haste to stop, even to help a countryman, or they saw us for what we were.

It didn't matter if they did by that point for I ordered the black flag to be raised and a shot fired across their bow. They were outnumbered and I had thought that they would have struck their colours, knowing that they could not outrun us. Don Miguel must have valued his cargo more than his life, or perhaps he feared what might become of the man who lost the queen's jewels, for he resisted, his men peppering us with grape shot from his swivels and firing at us with muskets.

I ordered the crew to return fire. We tore into her rigging with round shot, taking care not to hole her below the waterline. We grappled her and, through the stinking fug of powder smoke, we boarded her.

I had taken up the custom of carrying a pistol in my left hand and my cutlass in my right so that I might shoot the first person I came upon and then bring my cutlass to bear on the next or, if necessary, defend myself from any counterattack.

My pistol ball split the skull of a Spaniard as soon as I set foot on deck. The knowledge that I had killed my first man was heavy in my mind and my insides churned but there was no time to dwell on it for two men with pikes made to charge me. Adolpho was by my side, a red bandanna around his head and fury in his eyes. He pistoled one of the men while I engaged the other, our steel clattering and slithering as the two crews met around us in a hot, hacking fury.

My training with a blade served me well and I succeeded in cleaving my opponent through the shoulder, sending him reeling to the deck in a welter of blood. My crew were faring well against the Spaniards and there weren't many of them left by the time they struck their colours. I demanded the captain be brought before me.

Don Miguel, son of General Echeverz, was a short man dressed in the pompous finery I had come to expect from the Spaniards. As with the captain of the mail ship, I interrogated him in Spanish but he was of a much poorer temperament and refused to humour me.

"This ship belongs to the navy of His Catholic Majesty, King Felipe of Spain," he said in English, his face like thunder. "You have committed a gross act of piracy against a foreign nation and you will hang for it, I promise you."

"You're not quite in the position to make threats, *Don Miguel*."

He blinked, surprised that I knew his name.

"Yes, we have been waiting for you," I said. "And we know what it is you carry that speeds you on your way to Havana. Be so gracious as to fetch me the queen's jewels."

"I don't know what you're talking about," he said through gritted teeth.

"Oh, I think you do. And I'm afraid your king is going to have to keep a leash on his lust a little while longer. Now fetch them!"

My crew were already rummaging through the hold, opening chests and casks to see what we had scored. I doubted the precious jewels would be kept in the hold so I made my way to the Great Cabin, motioning to Walters to being the Spaniard along.

The cabin was small but well-appointed. I ordered every cupboard and locker broken open and rifled. Don

Miguel watched me with cold eyes while this was done and I held his gaze the whole time.

"Nothing, Captain," said Adolpho once the cabin had been truly ransacked.

"I'm losing my patience, Don Miguel," I said. "Either you tell me where the jewels are or I shall be forced to resort to more unpleasant tactics."

Truly I did not know what those tactics would be. Some pirates are not above torturing their prisoners to get information but such a thing had never crossed my mind. My hands still shook at my recent killing of two men. Killing was still a new experience in those days. I didn't know if I had it in me to actually torture someone and I hoped that the mere threat would be enough to convince my captive that I was in earnest, but I was to be disappointed.

"Go fuck yourself, you English whoreson!" Don Miguel told me, showing a rather colourful command of the English language.

I sighed. "Very well. Fetch him on deck in front of his crew."

Walters eyed me as Adolpho shoved and prodded the Spaniard out of the cabin with the muzzle of his pistol. He knew as well as I that I didn't have the first clue as to how to go about torturing somebody.

All eyes were upon us as we stepped out of the cabin. My men ringed the prisoners who were sitting in the waist and everybody present looked to me with expectant faces. I knew I could not disappoint them. I called Miguel over to translate my words to the prisoners.

"Now, the captain of this tub," I said, "refuses to tell me where his most precious cargo is held, namely a selection of jewels. This has forced me to dispense with all niceties and turn to extreme measures. Fetch rope to bind the captain!"

As Adolpho hurried off to carry out my orders, Walters spoke quietly in my ear.

"Are you sure you're up to this, Captain? If not, I could turn my hand to the bugger. Under Avery ..."

"That will be all, Walters," I said, perhaps a little harshly. But my crew recently had reason to question the quality of my leadership and, with experienced men like Walters under me, I had to ensure that they did not look to other prospects. I knew that if there was to be any torturing done to the captain, I would have to be the one to order it done else I risked losing face.

"Strip the prisoner down to his underclothes," I said.

Don Miguel's stoicism finally began to crack as Adolpho and Rogers ripped his clothes off him so that he stood before me in his shirt and underdrawers.

"What now, Captain?" Adolpho asked.

I had been thinking on that while the unfortunate Spaniard's clothes were being torn from his back and I was reminded of an old threat made to me, seemingly a lifetime ago, by Sam Spritnel in Bristol.

"I want him hanging from the rigging," I said. "By his thumbs."

Walters glanced at me and I could see the look of surprise in his eyes.

Grinning, Adolpho and some of the others obliged while the prisoners watched on, appalled. Soon, Don Miguel was dangling by his thumbs, his face screwed up in pain while his feet scrabbled in vain for the deck which was just out of reach. Still he refused to cooperate and an anger that I was not used to grew in my belly like an ugly storm cloud. I was angry that this man was making me do this. I was angry that his stubbornness was turning me into something I did not recognise or like. It is ironic that this very anger made me want to hurt him more.

Now, Sam Spritnel's measure called for a beating with a length of chain but I wanted something more showy and less blunt so I called for fuses to be tucked between Don Miguel's toes. Before I lit them, I waved the brand under his nose.

"Last chance before I set you burning like a candle," I told him. "Where are the jewels?"

He appeared to be too consumed by his own agony and fear to respond. Everybody was silent as I held the brand threateningly, wondering if I would really do it. I knew I could not back down now, so I knelt down and lit the fuses.

We all watched patiently as they burned down. Don Miguel seemed to be dragged out of his thoughts by the scorching between his toes and the stink of burning hair and skin drifted up to his nose.

"Stop! Stop! I beg you!" he yelled.

I knocked the fuses out from between his toes and they tumbled to the deck to be snuffed out by Walters and Adolpho.

"You'll talk?" I asked.

"You give me no choice!"

I smiled and nodded. "Not really, no."

We cut him down and had to help him hobble back to his cabin to show us where the jewels were hidden. He indicated a floorboard behind the captain's table and we fetched a crowbar to lever it up. In the recess lay a small lockbox. Lifting it out, I opened it and grinned when I saw that we had hit paydirt at last.

A heart lay within the chest. It was gold, about three inches across, and studded with pearls. A gold chain was attached to it, making it a pendant clearly intended to hang around the neck of Spain's new queen.

"Bloody hell!" Walters exclaimed.

"Think we'll be able to shift something like this in the kind of places we frequent?" I asked him.

"I think we could manage that," he replied.

There was some sort of commotion on deck and I sent Walters out to make sure all was well with the prisoners while I returned the golden heart to its box and secured it.

"Captain!" Walters called me from on deck.

We stepped outside and I saw that my quartermaster's face was pale with concern.

"What is it?" I asked him.

"Another Spaniard. A forty-gunner, bearing down on us from the north."

"Cut us loose," I said. "With an empty hold we can outrun some Spanish slug."

"It's a brigantine," Walters said. "Privateer, by the looks of her."

Don Miguel smiled at our exchange, as if he knew something we didn't. "The *Santa Teresa*. You think you can plunder these waters without drawing attention? Captain Antonio y Ramírez is one of our finest *guarda costas*. You will not escape him."

"Ramírez ..." I said to Walters.

"The fellow who took *La Cuerva*," he replied.

"Get us underway!" I yelled at the crew on deck.

To the north I could see the white sails of a large brigantine bellying as it came about. My crew scrambled to disengage us from *La Hollandesa*, abandoning the rest of the cargo that still lay in its hold. It mattered little to us; we had what we came for.

We left *La Hollandesa* to continue on its journey north while I had Walters and Harrison chart us a course northeast, into the curving arm of Cuba. I hoped that we might hide from this Captain Ramírez in the cays and islands on its leeward side, before slipping by him and heading up the Straits of Yucatán for Nassau.

They chased us for a day and we entered the string of cays and sandbars that I knew would be treacherous for a keel as deep as the *Santa Teresa's*. It was pretty hairy for us too and I had a man posted to plumb the depths at all times. We lost sight of our pursuer and had to hope that Captain Ramírez was not fool enough to follow us.

The Isle of Pines is uninhabited but often frequented by pirates for there is much timber to be had and plenty of game and fruit. We put in at an inlet on its northern side where another vessel was at anchor, its crew camped on the beach. It was a sloop of eight guns and, as there were no colours flying from either the ship or the camp, I assumed them to be pirates.

They were wary of us at first, but, upon learning that we were as motley in our mix of nationalities as they were, they invited us to drink with them, provided we brought something. I had two casks of Madeira brought ashore and we spent several days with our fellow brethren, sharing stories and news.

Their captain was a Frenchman by the name of Olivier Levasseur who had been a privateer during the war and, now cut loose, had turned to outright piracy with his captured sloop he had named *La Postillion*.

After a week or so had passed, I deemed it safe to leave the island and make for the Yucatán Straits. The *Santa Teresa* had surely moved on by now and we were keen to make what we could of the queen's jewels in Nassau.

Bidding farewell to Levasseur and his crew, we set out and noticed that the weather had turned considerably for the worse. It was going to be a choppy voyage north but, as we rounded the island, we realised that we had something worse to worry about. A large brigantine had been lurking on the other side of the island and it was now making for us with crowded sails.

"The *Santa Teresa*?" I asked Walters.

"Aye," he said, looking through his spyglass.

"Doesn't that Spanish bugger ever give up?"

I ordered every scrap of canvas thrown up but the wind was belting hard from the north-east. As we beat our way towards the straits, we could see a black cloud on the eastern horizon that seemed to swell with each passing second. It bulged out over the choppy whitecaps and the sky became tinged with a sickly yellow laden with potent energy. In the darkest parts of the oncoming cloud, we could see streaks of lightning.

"We'll have a job of it skirting that hell," Walters said. "Hurricane, or I'm a Dutchman."

"Keep our course," I said. "With any luck, the Spaniard will fall back and reef her sails rather than pursue us."

I snapped my spyglass open and looked back at our pursuer. She was still coming up fast. Our own sails bellied hard but it was becoming dangerous. The masts bent and the deck warped as the hurricane swept its great arms over the rising waves. Spots of rain pelted us and soon we were drenched as the sky blackened over our heads like a fresh bruise. The *Azrael* cut through the frothy bulges and sank alarmingly through the green troughs. She was struggling and the storm surges were gradually pushing her towards the distant green of the Yucatán coast.

"Captain, we must change course!" Walters yelled.

"No!" I cried. "Keep her steady! It's the only way to outrun that Spaniard!"

"What good will it do us if we are hurled against the shore like matchwood?"

I said nothing but I gripped the rail with whitened knuckles, stubborn in my belief that we would get through this. The *Santa Teresa* continued to chase us and I concluded that Captain Ramírez must be as mad as I was.

"She's dropped back!" Walters cried at last, looking astern. "She's reefing sail and changing course. Captain, we must do the same!"

"Haul all canvas in!" I yelled back. "Drop anchor!"

As our anchor plummeted towards the sea bottom, we battened down everything that might fly loose and made ready to weather the storm. The wind whipped and howled around our ears and the *Azrael* strained against her moorings. The rain hammered us and the surf pounded the shore like white hammers. The sky was black like premature night and all we could do was hold fast as the ship listed dangerously to larboard.

I went below to see if any food was to be had. The crew were huddled together in wet, frightened groups and the air was thick with the stink of vomit. The galley stove was lit and our replacement cook after Moon's departure was resolutely handing out pease pudding and rum.

I accepted a bowl and traversed the leaning deck, keen to get something warm inside me and a strong measure of rum to steady my nerves. Before I was able to sit down, there was a loud thud that shuddered through the ship and a great lurch as it listed even more to larboard. Men tumbled end over end and were hurled against the bulkheads. I was able to cling on and I heard Walters yell; "The moorings have snapped! We're drifting!"

I scrambled my way back on deck and surveyed the situation. The *Azrael* was twisting as she listed, her bow pointed at the coast. Harrison was at the wheel and I ran to help him.

"It's no use!" he yelled. "Bloody rudder's snapped!"

A cold dread opened up in the pit of my stomach. No rudder and the moorings gone. We were headed for the shore and there wasn't a damned thing we could do about it.

There was no sign of the *Santa Teresa*; either she was sunk or the hammering rain obscured her completely. I had other things to think about in any case as the grey shore loomed ever closer.

"Captain, we must abandon her and make for the shore in the longboats!" Walters cried.

I swore something fierce at the prospect of losing the *Azrael* but I knew that he was right. In the longboats, we had a chance of making the shore alive but aboard the *Azrael*, we would be hurled to our deaths.

"Lower them!" I said. "I must retrieve something from the cabin."

I had thought he might try to stop me for Walters was always the voice of reason but he knew what I was after and he said nothing. Both of us would rather go down with the *Azrael* than survive and lose the Molucca Star.

I fought my way to the cabin and entered to find everything in disarray. Stumbling over to the table, I reached beneath it for the lockbox that now contained both the queen's golden heart and the Molucca Star. The lockbox under my arm, I struggled to get back on deck but, before I made it to the doors, there was a great shudder that shook the *Azrael* to its beams.

I was knocked off my feet and swore loudly as I banged my shoulder and the lockbox went skittering behind a bulkhead. I knew that we had run aground and was thankful that the ship had not been smashed to matchwood. Staggering out on deck, I headed for the rail and cursed to see both longboats, perilously overloaded with men, heading for the shore which was a lot closer than it had been moments ago. I knew they would not have deserted me voluntarily – Walters would have shot any man who tried – so assumed the boats had been knocked free when the ship had pitched itself on this sandbar.

I was stuck aboard this dangerously tilting ship with no way of reaching either the shore or my comrades while the hurricane howled its rage about my ears. Blinking against the rain and whipping winds, I made my way back to the cabin to bolt the doors and try to weather the storm.

I crawled behind a bulkhead and hugged the lockbox tightly. God could do his worst as far as I was concerned. I would die in my cabin, aboard my own ship with the fortunes of a hundred men gripped tightly in my hands if I had to.

I slept a little, fitful and interrupted as the hurricane passed over the ship, causing it to creak and groan and, on several alarming occasions, shift in the sand. The more hours that passed increased my confidence that I might actually survive this wreck although what would become of me then I had no idea.

I awoke to find hot sunlight streaming in through the cabin windows and all noise gone but for the gentle lapping of small waves against the hull and the cawing of some birds. I got up and, the floor still pitched at a nauseating angle, made my way out on deck to survey the situation.

The storm was gone as if it had been nothing more than a waking nightmare. The shore was a lush green banded by white gold and the turquoise waves gently rolled up it, washing a great degree of wreckage from the *Azrael* upon the sand.

With both the longboats gone, I began to look around for some way to fashion a raft that would carry me and whatever cargo I could salvage to the shore. Before I had begun, I could hear voices hailing me and, opening my spyglass, I could see one of the longboats approaching from the south, Walters standing up in the stern, waving his arms at me. I waved back and grinned, pleased to see that some of my comrades at least had survived and were now coming to get me.

They moored at the port ladder which was the side of the ship that was lowest to the water and Walters came aboard. "Blasted good fortune the ship is whole," he told me. "I've seen better ships reduced to kindling before."

"How many men did we lose?" I asked him.

"Only three which is another stroke of mercy. The other longboat capsized but most of the crew were able to make it to shore. We stockpiled what flotsam we could and sheltered in the jungle a mile or so down the coast. We had a bad night of it with palms bending like whips around us. How was yours?"

"Slept like a babe," I lied.

We ventured down into the hold to see what we might salvage from our stores. Water lapped at our feet and we knew the *Azrael* had been holed somewhere. We fished out as much as the longboat could carry and then made our way to shore.

"If we pull her ashore we might be able to make her seaworthy yet," Walters said to me.

"You think so?" I asked.

"Given time. And time is something we may find ourselves overburdened with on this stretch of coast. The Yucatán is one of the wildest and most untamed parts of the Caribbean. The nearest European settlement are the British logwood cutters of Belize Town which, to my reckoning, lies damn near two-hundred miles to the south."

"Two-hundred miles of dense jungle populated only by savages," Rogers put in. "I say we stay put and work on the ship."

My crew were pleased to hear that both their captain and their ship had survived and we spent the rest of the day building a camp on the shore and ferrying stores from the *Azrael*. We managed to salvage several barrels of salt pork, rum and biscuit but the flour had all been spoiled and much of the powder was wet. We set the latter to drying in the sun but our biggest problem was lack of water. A few of our casks had been smashed by the storm and we had very little left. I sent men into the jungle to find a river or a spring but they came back at nightfall with nothing.

This was a great concern to us for, though the jungle might provide us with much game and fruit, without water we would perish within days. The following morning, I formed two parties, one to go north up the coast and the other to go south, to look for water. I led the north party and before noon we spotted some buildings poking out of the jungled hillsides which at first filled us with joy for we believed we had come upon a settlement. As we drew closer, our hearts sank as we could see that they were nothing but the crumbling ruins of some dead native city.

We clambered up the rocky, palm-dotted cliffs to where the ancient city stood and looked out across the vast blue sea to our right and the deep gloom of the jungle to our left. Here we were, penned between two infinite and impenetrable dooms.

We poked about in the ruins and marvelled at what had once been a populated city now nothing but shattered remains half swallowed by the jungle. The largest building must have been some sort of temple for it had a wide staircase up one side that led to a vaulted chamber at the top with a view of the ocean. Other buildings which must have once had roofs of thatch lay open to the sky, warped and twisted by tree roots. Statues and monuments carved with the images of serpents and winged pagan gods dotted the site, the forgotten guardians of this place of ghosts.

"I don't like this place," Rogers said. "It ain't holy."

"I didn't think savages were capable of such constructions," I said.

"They were once," said Walters. "The Spaniards put an end to that. Now they're all dead or dispersed by war and disease. The natives who live in the jungles of Yucatán are the descendants of this devilish race and even they shun this place, most like."

We found no water and were left to wonder how the inhabitants of this city had slaked their thirst. There may have been some spring or river further into the jungle, any path to it long since overgrown. But Walters' talk of savages in the jungle robbed us of any courage to penetrate that green gloom further and we all wanted to leave the place and return to the camp.

When we got back, we found that the other exploration party had also returned.

"Good news and bad," Harrison said, for I had made him the leader of that party. "The good news is that there is water nearby. The bad news is that it's guarded."

"Guarded?" I exclaimed. My hand went to the butt of my pistol and several others in my party did the same, our fears of nearby savages heightening.

"It appears that the Spaniards survived the storm also and were washed into a bay about three miles south of here. Their ship is in a poor state, heeled over with her mainmast snapped, but there are at least a hundred Spaniards encamped there. We spied on them from the cliffs and watched as they brought casks of water from some source hidden in the jungle."

"Blast it!" I said.

"There's too many of them for us to overcome, even if we take them by surprise," said Harrison.

"And that source of water might be the only one for miles around," added Walters.

"We have a bigger problem than that," I said. "We're both going to be on this stretch of shore for quite a while. There's no way we can remain undetected for long."

"What should we do?" asked Walters.

I rubbed my chin. "Walters," I said. "Fix me up a flag of truce. We're going to pay our neighbours a visit."

"Surrender?" Walters exclaimed.

"Certainly not. But I have a plan that might allow us access to whatever water they've found."

I selected a group of men which included Walters, Adolpho and Miguel and we headed south along the coast holding a white flag on a palm stave high enough to be seen at a distance. The Spaniards had already constructed an impressive camp with sailcloth tents, stockpiles of supplies and several cookfires. They had something of a perimeter made from driftwood where men with muskets were posted. They were clearly afraid of attack and that played into my plan nicely.

Cries went up at our approach and there was a tense few moments as both sides glared at each other, unsure who was going to make the first move. I ordered my men not to draw weapons which was a tall order in the face of a score of Spanish muzzles pointed at us.

"I wish to speak with your captain," I said in my best Spanish. "We come in peace to discuss terms."

Captain Antonio Ramírez came forward; a flamboyantly dressed man and I had no cause to expect otherwise, but there was more of the pirate about him than the militaristic uniforms of the other Spanish captains I had met. He wore a white calico shirt with a sash of red silk about his waist, black breeches tucked into boots of Spanish leather and a deal of gold ornamentation about his ears and neck.

"Captain Ramírez?" I enquired.

He seemed pleased that I knew his name and he surprised me by returning my own.

"Captain Rake of the *Azrael*. It is a pleasure to finally meet you in the flesh."

"How do you know me, sir?"

"I had your name from the lips of one Thomas Moon, a pirate who briefly commanded the Spanish ship *La Cuerva*. I was dispatched to hunt him down for his part in the murder of my fellow privateer, Captain Luis de Polanco and the theft of his ship. I had been told by my countrymen who had been deserted on Saint Thomas that two ships had left with all the sugar from the Ensomhed plantation and I had hoped to capture both. I was disappointed to find that the two vessels had parted ways, but Mr. Moon was very quick to name you as his associate and provided a good description of your ship."

There was grumbling at my back from Walters and the others at Moon's cowardice but it hardly mattered now. Here we were, shipwrecked on the same coast and our only chance at survival lay in building some bridges with our former pursuers.

"You are quite the hunter, Captain Ramírez," I said. "You gave us a good chase but it was perhaps my own folly not to strike my colours before that storm took us."

He smiled. "I thought you a madman to continue on your course and it was a bitter draught for me to give up the chase and admit defeat, though it was too late in any case. Now we are both marooned here."

"Yes," I said. "And perhaps there is sense in us banding together rather than remaining enemies."

He laughed. "You, sir, are an English pirate and I am a Spanish privateer in the service of His Catholic Majesty. Do not mistake my admiration of your courage as a sign of friendship. There can be no alliance between us."

"Come now, Captain. We are far removed from the world of politics now. Only our survival in a harsh land matters. Together we might stand a chance against the savages that infest these jungles. I have forty men along with powder and shot to give a good account of ourselves. But there is further strength to be had in unity, no?"

My mention of savages had the Spaniards in a fluster.

"You saw some?" Captain Ramírez said, casting fearful eyes to the jungle atop the cliffs that surrounded the beach. "Close to here?"

"A small scouting party," I lied. "But they will report to their chief that we are here and may return in force. We should be ready."

Captain Ramírez cleared his throat. "You speak sense, Englishman. Perhaps it is wise for us to put our differences behind us and join forces. How is your ship?"

"In better shape than yours but beached on a sandbar."

"Then we are both stranded here for the foreseeable future. Have you many stores?"

"Some but we need water. It looks like you have found some."

"Indeed. There is a cenote about three miles inland."

"A cenote?"

"A natural sinkhole in the bedrock that exposes groundwater. I will take you to it so that you may replenish your stores."

"Much obliged, Captain."

"And I suggest you move your camp closer to ours so we might be better prepared should the savages attack."

"Agreed."

"That was a cunning move," Walters said to me as we headed back to our camp. "Telling them that you saw some savages."

"We have little to bargain with but guns and manpower," I replied. "Which he also has in abundance. I just made him value numbers a little higher."

"Do you think we can work side by side with the Spaniards without killing each other?"

"We'll have to try. This captain of theirs seems like a sensible type. At least we're not stuck with somebody like Don Luis."

We fetched plenty of men and as many whole casks as we could put together and returned to the Spanish camp. Captain Ramírez led us on a thirsty trek through the humid jungle to this cenote he had spoken of.

We found it to be a tranquil lagoon surrounded by mangrove trees, the water bluer than any I had ever seen. It truly was a piece of Eden in that steaming and tangled jungle. We slaked our thirst and filled up our water casks.

"Cenotes like this are hundreds of years old," Captain Ramírez said. "The Mayans used them for their water."

"Mayans?" I asked. "Are they the people who built cities on this peninsula?"

"Yes. They once ruled this land like kings but now they are gone and their cities lie in ruins."

"I have seen some of these ruins. To the north of our camp there are some that look like they were once a city."

"Really? I would like to see these."

"I'll take you to them. But first, we must get these casks back to camp and see to our defences."

It was a long and hard trek back to the coast loaded down with our casks and it was dark by the time we saw the campfires on the beach. We left our casks at the Spanish camp while we moved our own camp closer to theirs. There was still much scepticism from both sides but the imagined eyes watching us from the darkened jungle put the fear of God into most of the men so that even the company of traditional enemies provided some comfort.

We ate and drank with the Spaniards that night and did our best to become better acquainted. We knew that whatever liquor had been salvaged from the ships would have to be strictly rationed but both I and Captain Ramírez felt that the evening called for a little indulgence to better facilitate the forming of friendships.

I drank with Captain Ramírez in the large sailcloth tent that had been erected for his use. Our conversation (and my Spanish) was lubricated somewhat by rum, and

I found him to be a likeable fellow and it was clear to me that his crew held him in high regard.

"So you bear me no ill feelings for the death of Don Luis de Polanco?" I said, at length, keen to test the waters further. I was careful not to implicate myself in Polanco's death for in truth, it was not I who pulled the trigger, but I wasn't going to implicate Adolpho either.

"I knew Don Luis," Captain Ramírez told me. "We both sailed under the mulatto privateer Don Miguel Enríquez, and, although I was honour-bound to hunt you down, I bear no man a grudge for killing such a corrupt degenerate. His loyalties lay only in himself. Little wonder you found him selling slaves to a Dane."

"I am glad you feel that way," I said. "For we may be sharing this beach for quite some time."

"As long as you keep your men in order, I do not foresee a problem. We can share resources, tools, even manpower, the amicability of our respective crews permitting."

"I hope that will be the case," I replied. "It will take us many weeks to repair our ships but we may help each other escape this desolate stretch of coast alive." I held up my drinking jack. "To our alliance."

"I will drink to that!" he replied, toasting me in return. "If your command over your men is a match for your brazen courage, you would have made a fine *guarda costa* had you been born a Spaniard!"

"I thank you, Captain."

"But you were born an Englishman and so I must call you a pirate."

"One man's privateer is another man's pirate," I said.

"Those waters have been muddied in recent years it is true," he said. "But there is still an important distinction between the two."

"And that is?"

"Whether your own nation considers you a privateer or a pirate depends entirely on what you do with your prizes. Do you keep them for yourself or do you take them to your admiralty courts?"

It may have been a rhetorical question but I felt like answering it anyway. "I owe no allegiance to my country," I said. "Its courts tried to hang me and my brothers a long time ago. I swear allegiance to no flag but the black."

"So, a pirate then, not a privateer. And the queen's pearl-studded heart is to be sold or broken up and shared among your crew."

His sudden revelation that he knew what lay in my strongbox caught me off guard. He saw my expression and laughed, a little too loud, as if he were trying to dispel the sudden tension.

"I gave aid to the ship you robbed and helped her on her way to Havana," he explained. "The rather ashamed captain gave an account of your actions, including what you took from him. From my queen I should say. Your possession of it encouraged me to hunt you as much as the avenging of Don Luis."

I said nothing.

"Oh, relax, Captain Rake. I am merely teasing you. Come, let us call for more rum. Our stores won't last so we might as well drink it as quickly as possible so the men will know it is gone and will not thirst for it day after day."

He bellowed for more to be brought and I silently warned myself that I would have to be careful. *He wants that jewel*, I thought. And I knew that the friendship we had so recently struck depended entirely on our mutual interest in survival. Once our ships were repaired, he would try to take it from me in the name of his queen, I had no doubt of that. *Still*, I tried to comfort myself. *At least he knows nothing of the Molucca Star, which is the far greater treasure in my possession.*

The next day, with sore heads, we set to work. First, we salvaged the wreckage of the other longboat which had washed ashore along with the three dead men whom we buried with due ceremony. The longboat repaired, we sent both out to the *Azrael* and began stripping her of her guns and other weighty items so that we might move her with more ease. Walters took a couple of men aboard and made some rudimentary repairs to her gashed side to prevent her sinking when we tried to move her.

Lightened by her load, the *Azrael* bobbed upright with the incoming tide, and we were pleased to see that Walters' repairs were holding, at least for a while. Using the longboats and the rising tide, we pulled her free from the sandbank and into shallow waters where we anchored her and waited for the tide to go out so that we might heel her over onto her undamaged side. Anchored in place with moorings on her masts, the damaged portion of the hull would always be exposed, even at high tide, enabling us to make our repairs.

A couple of days later, I took Captain Ramírez to the ruined Mayan city. He was most intrigued and we explored the whole site together, discussing its suitability as a fortification.

"It is perfectly situated for defence against sea invaders," he said. "These steep cliffs and high walls make it near impenetrable. The Mayans certainly knew what they were doing and imagine if we could winch cannons into position! We would be invulnerable to attack."

"From the sea," I said. "But the site is less defensible against attack from the jungle." I wanted to keep the threat of savages in the forefront of his mind. We had seen no sign of them and I was worried that he might begin to suspect that I had lied to him.

"True, true," he said. "Ah! It is all just for conversation in any case. We are safe enough on the beach and I want to concentrate our efforts on repairing our ships rather than waste time fortifying this place. Still, it is fun to imagine, eh?"

"Aye," I agreed. But I believed that Captain Ramírez had other reasons for not wanting to move into the ruins for I shared those same reasons. Neither of us wanted to admit to the other that the thought of living in this place of ghosts frightened us.

"When all this is over and we are free of this place," he said, "what do you say to coming to Santo Domingo with me and working for the Spanish Crown? We always have need of good men with good ships. My brother is governor there and he will open many doors to you."

I knew his game. He was keener to bring the Spanish queen's jewelled heart to Santo Domingo than me. "Is your brother really the governor of Santo Domingo?" I asked him.

"Yes. A stoic old buffoon but a loyal one. We are as different as chalk and cheese though we serve the same masters."

"I thank you for the offer," I said. "But my crew are mostly Englishmen and, pirates they may be, I doubt they'd be keen to serve Spain."

"We are at peace, man! And are you saying that pirates who prey on their own country's shipping are too high and mighty to serve a country they were once at war with?"

"Well, that's just it. Many of my men fought in the war on privateers and naval vessels. They fought and bled against Spanish guns and lost many comrades. They may have forsaken their own country but bad feelings are much harder to dispel than oaths of loyalty to a country they feel has misused them."

"Fair enough," he said with a sigh. "I suppose we must eventually fall back into our own places in the world. I just hope that we are not forced to fight each other in the future."

Weeks passed with nothing but hard toil to occupy our minds. Hunting parties went out and occasionally shot deer and fowl. They found no pigs; swine being unknown to those parts. We guarded our powder and shot preciously, relying primarily on trapping and fishing. Occasionally turtles would come ashore and they made very good eating, cooked in the way of the buccaneers by roasting them in their shells beneath the sand.

Work progressed well on our respective ships, though it was slow going. We pooled resources and built a sawmill and felled many trees for the shaping of planks. The weather was temperamental, dousing us in sudden rains that passed on as quickly as they came and the winds were something fierce at times. The thought of putting out to sea in hurricane season was not a pleasing prospect, even if we did get our ships seaworthy before November.

By and large, our respective crews got along. Occasional fights broke out, usually over misunderstandings and the division of supplies, but there was no significant bloodshed. As the months passed, we began to feel a sense of unity but I constantly reminded myself of the danger of getting comfortable with someone who would be my enemy under any other circumstances. I knew what Captain Ramírez truly wanted and no amount of banding together and shared resources would fool me into thinking otherwise.

As November approached and our ships were close to completion, an incident happened that convinced me that haste was now required. It was Solomon who came to me, his face greatly concerned.

"Captain, may I have a word in private?" he asked me.

"What's the trouble?" I said, leading him to a quiet spot between the lean-tos we had constructed out of lumber and palm thatch that served as our sleeping quarters.

"It's Fiaschetti," he said. "He's killed a savage."

"He's what!" I hissed, now understanding Solomon's request for privacy. The very notion that savages might indeed be close by would be enough to throw both camps into a panic. "Where?"

"We were hunting about a mile inland. Fiaschetti was squatting in a thicket when he saw the man pass by. He must have been a scout for we saw no others. He had seen Gunderson and myself and was creeping up on us, or so Fiaschetti says."

"So he shot him?"

"Aye, Captain. Right through the chest."

"What have you done with the body?"

"Fiaschetti and Gunderson are with it now. We thought it best to tell you before we did anything."

"Very wise. If anybody else gets wind of this – especially the Spaniards – we might have a panic on our hands. Take me to the body."

We surreptitiously fetched some shovels and headed off through the jungle as quickly as we could. We came upon Fiaschetti and Gunderson in a shallow dip, standing over the lifeless form of the slain man.

He was naked but for a loincloth and sandals. His jet-black hair was long and held up in an extraordinary ponytail. Several tattoos marked his coppery skin and he was adorned with jewellery fashioned from beads and bone. There was an ugly hole in the left side of his breast, just below his heart and blood seeped through the loam beneath him. His dead eyes gazed up at the wavering canopy of leaves.

"Well, your marksmanship is to be commended, Fiaschetti," I told my Italian crewman. "But this puts us into quite a spot."

"Aye, if this fellow's companions learn of his death, we might have a whole tribe of them falling upon us," said Gunderson, a large Swede we had picked up in Nassau.

"We must bury the body," I said. "Deep so that the scavengers do not rake him up." I tossed Fiaschetti a shovel. "Get digging."

Solomon and I stood watch while Fiaschetti and Gunderson buried the body as deep as we felt we had time for. We covered the grave with leaves and did our best to make it as inconspicuous as possible.

"That'll have to do," I said. "Not a word of this to anyone. I'm thinking mostly of your own safety, Fiaschetti."

The Italian gazed at me uncomprehendingly.

"If we do come under attack in retaliation for this killing," I explained, "then folks will most likely not be so pleased to learn that it was you who brought it upon us."

Comprehension dawned and Fiaschetti nodded in agreement.

The incident, although dealt with, had put me on edge. I had lied to Captain Ramírez about savages in the woods but now that I knew it was a fact, I was keen to get underway as soon as possible. The hurricane season was nearly over and our ships were in good standing, their hulls and masts repaired, new spars fitted and sails patched. The *Azrael* had a new rudder and all that really remained was the loading of our guns and the reprovisioning.

It was mid-November by the time we finally began loading the *Azrael*. Captain Ramírez was spurred on by this, realising that our time together on the coast of Yucatán was coming to a close. He quickly got his men in order and began resupplying his own ship which was fully repaired and at anchor not far from the *Azrael*.

While we had been friends for the better part of four months, the sudden dawning of our departures brought a return to the suspicion and distrust of our earliest days. As soon as we were out on the open sea, we would no longer be companions banding together in the interest of safety. We would be enemies – pirates and *guarda costas* – and I knew that Captain Ramírez would not hesitate to attack and board us to get his hands on the queen's heart.

The division in our camp was almost immediate. Now that we had our ships, we no longer had to share the beach and the stretch of water between our vessels, small it may have been, was as good as an ocean. A curious form of stalemate developed with each crew waiting for the other to make the first move. I knew that Captain Ramírez would not leave first but I knew also that as soon as we put out to sea, the *Santa Teresa* would open fire on us. So we waited while both captains contemplated this conundrum.

In the end it was Captain Ramírez who offered the olive branch. He came aboard the *Azrael* one fine morning to speak with me.

"The stormy season has passed and we are both in good shape to put out to sea," he said. "Let us celebrate the end of our brief partnership on the beach tonight before we say farewell to it and to each other. I have a one barrel of Madeira left and I believe you have saved some rum, am I right?"

"Little enough but yes," I admitted. I had saved some rum and it had been many weeks since any of my crew had tasted a drop.

"Fine! Let us and our crews drink the last of it for soon enough we will reach ports where liquor will flow like water once more!"

"Agreed," I said. "We all deserve a little merriment after our months of hard work."

He seemed pleased with this and I, fool that I am, believed it to be genuine. After all, we had got along surprisingly well during our time together and I mistakenly thought that he felt some sorrow at our imminent parting.

How wrong I was.

Our party was as raucous as our limited supply of liquor allowed. With the knowledge that we would be gone from this godforsaken shore by tomorrow, we drank everything and gorged ourselves on food we were not planning on bringing with us. I was enjoying myself so much that I didn't realise a member of my crew had gone missing.

Captain Ramírez was in his element, playing the host as most of the tents and stores left on the beach were his. He appeared to drink as much as I did but upon later reflection, I must conclude that it was feigned. He toasted me and my crew and thanked us for being such good comrades over the past few months. I should have realised right then that something was amiss but I was so caught up in the celebrations that my usual keen wits were somewhat dulled.

"It really is a shame you refused my offer of employment in the service of His Catholic Majesty," Captain Ramírez told me. "I've grown to like you, Rake, and it pains my heart to have to leave you here."

"I'll be sailing out on the same tide as you, Ramírez," I replied.

"I'm afraid you won't. The *Azrael* is smaller than the *Santa Teresa* but she is still capable of delivering a crippling broadside."

"Why would she?" I asked, feeling for the first time that something was wrong. "We are friends, are we not?"

"I dearly wish us to remain so but I fear, after tonight, you will do your utmost to destroy me."

The gathering of pirates and Spanish privateers had fallen silent. My crew blinked at one another, not sure of what was going on.

"I don't follow you, Ramírez," I said, my hand absently feeling for the butt of my pistol.

Captain Ramírez gave me a sad smile and reached into a sack that lay at his feet. What he drew out of that sack stunned me into a silent pillar of fury. It was my lockbox or at least, its identical twin. Captain Ramírez gave it a shake and the sound of the items rattling within left me with no doubt that it was my lockbox containing the queen's heart and the Molucca Star. I felt sick, like the world had flipped upside down around me.

"How ..." I managed.

"How did I get it?" Captain Ramírez said. "Merely turned one of your crew to my side. He took it from your cabin while we made merry here. Don't think too badly of him. It is only natural that he should wish to return to his own nation, given the chance."

"I am sorry, Captain," Miguel said and for the first time I noticed that he was standing at Captain Ramírez's side. "He promised me a pardon from the Spanish king and reward enough to set myself up as a wealthy man in Santo Domingo."

My eyes spat fire at the turncoat. As soon as Captain Ramírez said that I was betrayed, my mind reeled through a list of possibilities but the small, mild-mannered Spaniard who had taught me so much and had been one of my inner circle, had been farthest from my mind.

"So, you see, my English friend," Captain Ramírez went on, "the *Santa Teresa* and the *Azrael* will sail on the dawn tide but you and your crew must remain on this beach. We will leave you with provisions and, now that the hurricane season has passed, I am sure you will be able to make yourselves known to a passing ship. I will take good care of the *Azrael*, you have my word as a gentleman. She will make a fine addition to the *guarda costas* even if you will not."

My pistol was out of my sash and cocked before any Spaniard knew what I was doing. I knew that our only chance lay in acting fast and surprising these men who meant to maroon us. Unfortunately, such haste does not give adequate time to take proper aim and my shot – which I aimed at Captain Ramírez's head – went wide.

But the signal was given to my men that I meant to fight and, as the Spaniards fell back in surprise and their captain hurled himself to the sand, they brought their own weapons to bear.

Shots cracked out in the light of the cookfires and several Spaniards fell. I dove for cover behind a stack of provisions meant for the longboats and hurriedly reloaded my pistol. I could hear Captain Ramírez barking at his men in Spanish and I risked a glance from behind my cover. I could not see him but Miguel, that damnable turncoat, was making fast tracks away from the fight. I took aim with my pistol and felled him with a ball in his spine that hurled him forwards to land face down on the sand, never to betray anybody again.

"There's too many of them, Captain!" I heard Walters cry from his own cover. "And we have not the powder nor shot to hold them off indefinitely!"

"We must make for the longboats!" I called back.

To bolt from our cover was to be shot down like rabbits so I quickly called on the names of several men I knew would not waver in a firefight and bade them remain with me to provide covering fire while the rest of the crew ran for the boats. I ordered any spare pistols to be sent forth so we might give a good account of ourselves.

With two loaded pistols in my hands and a third at my feet, I peeped from behind my cover again. I could see the bodies of two of my men stretched on the sand, blood seeping from them. The Spaniards had taken cover by the tents and behind what remained of the barricades. A Spanish musket blazed and I ducked as a ball thudded into my cover. This was going to be a risky move but it was the only thing we could do. I swore that once we were back aboard the *Azrael*, Hell would freeze over before I allowed Captain Ramírez to escape with our fortune.

"On my signal!" I called to my men. "The rest of you, run like the devil is at your heels for in truth he will be!"

Silence reigned and the air was laden with expectancy.

"Now!" I yelled, rising from my cover and pointing my pistols in the direction of the Spaniards.

Almost immediately, the flash of a musket stabbed the darkness and I fired back at it, not knowing if I had hit my mark. Gunfire broke out all around me and the rest of my men took to their heels in the direction of the boats. I fired with my other pistol and succeeded in felling a Spaniard who rose to take aim at one of my comrades.

Ducking back down, I tossed my spent pistols to the sand and grasped my remaining one. I looked over my shoulder and could see my men pushing the longboats down into the surf. One or two of them had retrieved muskets and were firing back at the Spaniards.

Enemy fire had slowed as they reloaded their weapons.

"Now's our chance!" I yelled to the rest of my men. "For the boats!"

They took off, keeping their heads low as enemy shots broke out once more. Squatting on my haunches, I peered around my cover and tried to pick out a target to spend my final shot on.

"Captain, we must go!" Walters yelled.

"Don't wait for me!" I called back. "Get to those boats!"

The Spaniards were beginning to creep out from behind their cover and give chase. I stood up swiftly and felled one of them with my last shot. The Spaniards hurled themselves flat and I turned and ran.

Walters was by me, turning to fire off a last shot in the enemy's direction. I don't know if he hit anyone but it kept them back while we pelted for the boats, splashing into the surf and swimming out to them.

We were helped aboard and squirmed ourselves over the side as shots were fired from the shore. My men rowed for all their might while those with muskets fired back, making the boats rock precariously.

Once aboard the *Azrael* we felt safer but only a little. The *Santa Teresa* could sink us if she needed to but not without receiving a good peppering of round shot and I hoped that Captain Ramírez was still keen to get away unscathed. I ordered the guns run out in any case and made a show to anybody watching from the shore that we were beating to quarters.

We watched the Spaniards strike camp and make for the *Santa Teresa*. It was a tense few hours, all of us waiting for the boom of cannons. But the *Santa Teresa* made no move to set sail. Our two ships rode at anchor, their guns upon each other, the stalemate resumed with an added layer of deadly tension.

Walters and I were at the stern, watching the stars and the wavering palms of the night-cloaked shore wondering what we were to do when Walters cried; "A boat is putting out from the *Santa Teresa*!"

I grabbed the glass from my quartermaster and took a look at the launch setting out from the Spanish brigantine.

"I see Captain Ramírez," I said. "And a dozen men. What's he forgotten ashore, I wonder?"

We watched for the best part of an hour as the little boat was beached and the Spaniards waded ashore. They headed north along the beach and past the remnants of our own camp.

"Where the devil is he off to?" Walters said.

"The ruins!" I said with sudden excitement as our adversary's plan came into focus in my mind. "He means to fortify them!"

"With a dozen men and no guns?"

"He's probably just scouting them for now, making his plans. And with us aboard the *Azrael*, there isn't much we can do if he chooses to ferry his guns ashore along with a hundred men. We could try and stop him of course, but it would be a bloody fight and the *Santa Teresa* would undoubtedly fire upon us."

"If he places guns in that fort ..." Walters said.

"We would be caught between two batteries," I finished for him.

"By God, we've got to do something!"

"Aye, and the time is now. Lower one of the boats on the larboard side, out of view from the *Santa Teresa*. Walters, pick out a score of our best fighters and kit them out with pistols and cutlasses."

"We're going to storm Captain Ramírez and his party?" Walters asked. "We would outnumber them on land, it is true, but the *Santa Teresa* ..."

"Won't know anything about it," I said. "We'll let our Spanish friend enter the ruins and then fall upon them under the cover of night. Surprise will give us an extra edge and if we take Captain Ramírez hostage ..."

"We could buy back what he stole from us as well as our passage out of here!"

"Exactly."

We worked quickly and silently and, before Captain Ramírez and his men had vanished into the jungled cliffs at the feet of the ruined city, I was sitting in the stern of the longboat with twenty hardened pirates at my back. Walters was with me, as was Adolpho and Rogers. We slipped our cable and rowed ashore, screened for the most part by the *Azrael*.

Running the boat ashore, we hurried for the trees, hoping that the Spaniards were not keeping a close eye on the moonlit beach. The jungle was black and dense, the night air thick beneath the leafy canopy. Nocturnal animals hooted and growled as we pushed our way through, working our way up the steep cliffs to the Mayan city.

The moonlight made silver spectres of the ruins and I could not have been the only one who felt a shiver down my spine despite the warm night air. If this was a place of ghosts during the day, then it was a spot of nightmares at night. I tried not to think of the images of snakes and winged demons that had been carved into the stones all around us by hands long-dead.

We could see a torchlight wavering about up ahead, partially screened by tangled vines and chunks of fallen masonry. Keeping low, and with pistols drawn, we crept towards them. I could see the plumed tricorne of Captain Ramírez and I levelled my pistol at it, stepping out from behind cover. My men did the same and we caught the Spaniards unawares.

Or, so we thought.

"Captain Ramírez!" I said, flashing a grin. "You've gambled away your advantage. Foolish to come here with so few men in full view of the *Azrael*."

"It was a gamble, I must admit, Captain Rake," he replied. "But one that has paid off. For one of us came with too few men and it was not me."

At a signal, several figures rose from behind a fallen column at the Spaniard's back. Muskets were levelled at us and I knew then that we had walked into a trap.

"I sent twenty of my men to hide in these ruins before I returned with the rest of my crew to the *Santa Teresa*," Captain Ramírez explained. "I then made sure that you could see me rowing ashore and heading up to the ruins and you fell for the bait like dogs! You thought to fall upon me when I was vulnerable and ... what? Not kill me, I trust. No, you want that lockbox back, don't you?"

I said nothing.

"My dear Captain Rake. I had hoped to claim the jewel you stole from my queen but when I smashed the

214

lock on that box and found that other item within, I must confess I nearly lost my senses! Where did a sea rat like you come across such a fabulous diamond? You are quite mad to sail with it for I imagine that any man of your crew would gladly slit your throat for it and that's not to mention the risk of losing it to boarders or in a storm like the one that carried us here. You sat on this incredible treasure these months we have been together and said nothing of it? I am almost upset by such distrust!"

I was aware of the eyes of my crew on me. Other than Walters, Rogers, Harrison and Solomon, none of them knew what 'fabulous diamond' Captain Ramírez was talking about. Concealing booty from a crew was a big mistake for a captain as it went against the articles and could see one hanged for it. I had, in all good faith, planned to share the wealth with my crew once the troublesome diamond was sold but Ramírez was right; I hadn't trusted my crew to tell them of it. Now, I might be undone by that lack of trust.

"Where is it?" I demanded.

"Safely aboard the *Santa Teresa*," Ramírez replied with a grin. "Where you will be soon be joining it. I require your presence aboard to ensure my safe passage. Your men love you enough to not open fire on me, I trust?"

I said nothing.

"I really am being quite generous, I hope you realise this. Were the circumstances different, I would take you with me to Havana where your piratical career would meet its conclusion at the end of a rope. But, as we have been something akin to friends these past few months, I will put you off on the Isle of Pines where fellow men in your profession might find you and reunite you with your crew. If there is any attempt by the *Azrael* to interfere in my journey to Havana, then I will not hesitate to hang you from the yardarm before obliterating your ship with a full broadside."

I ground my teeth in fury.

"I see that you understand me," Ramírez said. "Now, if ..."

His words were cut short as something long and dark streaked out from the jungle and lodged in the neck of one of the Spaniards atop the fallen column. Captain Ramírez hadn't noticed for his back was to the stricken man but I and my crew watched him waver, his musket slipping from his hands as he reached up to clutch at his skewered neck. Blood pumped from the wound and between his lips. His knees buckled and, before he toppled from the column, three more men had been struck.

"Savages!" the Spaniards began to cry, turning this way and that, aiming their guns at the darkness which seemed to mask a legion of devils.

Captain Ramírez flung himself flat as I and my crew dove for cover too. The shouts of the war party that had fallen upon us echoed all around the abandoned city; the living giving voice to the ghosts of their ancestors.

Flashes of gunfire crackled in the darkness as the Spaniards fought back but more and more of them fell to arrows shot from hidden bows. We were surrounded and, with the cliffs at our backs, it seemed as we were like fish in a barrel.

"Blasted good timing," Walters yelled to me over the din of slaughter and war cries. "We're free from

Ramírez but how long we have to enjoy it, God alone knows!"

"They're in a rare state!" Rogers yelled on my other side. "Must have known about our presence here for this is no scouting party!"

"My guess is that they discovered the man Fiaschetti shot," I called back.

Both men goggled at me in the moonlight.

"I'll explain later but I doubt this attack is down to mere chance. Now, how the hell are we to get out of this?"

A figure scrambled over the broken wall and we pointed our weapons at him, fully expecting to see the dark face of a savage grinning death upon us, but it was Ramírez, torn and bloodied.

Some instinct to preserve the life of a fellow white man stayed our hands and we did not shoot him down, enemy though he was.

"It's a massacre!" he cried. "Half my men are slain and the other half fight on but it is no use! We are surrounded and these wild men keep on coming! We slew over a dozen but God knows how many there are out there!"

"Our only way out is down the cliffs to the beach," I said. "But the minute we break from cover, a hundred arrows will feather us."

"And we cannot remain here for long," Walters said. "Once those Spaniards are overwhelmed, the savages will be upon us with their axes!"

"Two groups in tandem," I said. "We fight a running battle to the cliffs and hope they don't pursue us down to the beach."

I looked at the faces of my men, pale with fear in the shadows.

"Courage, men," I told them. "I don't think their cordon reaches all the way to the cliffs to our left. If half of us crawl into the trees and form up, we can cover the escape of the other half. Then, when the savages fall back to take cover from our fusillade, the rest of us can make to the cliffs. It will be a devilishly fast scramble down to the beach but once we hit the sand we make for the boat with all haste. Agreed?"

There was a chorus of 'Aye, Captain' and nodding heads.

"I will lead the first group. Walters, you take the second. As soon as we open fire or wave you some other signal, get the men running."

"Aye, Captain," Walters said.

"I will go with Mr. Walters," said Ramírez, cocking his freshly loaded pistol. "I'll help him get your men to your boat."

"You'll stay with me, damn you," I snapped. "And hand me that pistol. I wouldn't trust you with a tinderbox at this point."

"You think to leave me unarmed in the face of these savages!" Ramírez cried.

"You'll die with us if worse comes to worst," I said. "One more pistol isn't likely to make much difference in any case. Right, you lot. Follow me!"

Our pistols and muskets gripped in sweaty hands, we crawled on our bellies across the sward, mostly concealed by the long grass. Further inland, the battle still raged between the attackers, and the Spaniards Ramírez seemed content to leave to their fates so we were able to make the treeline without being detected.

Kneeling at the edge of the jungle, we took up positions and trained our guns on the distant figures we caught only the barest glimpses of by moonlight and flash of gunpowder. As I was about to give the signal to Walters and his group to make for the cliffs, I was aware of Ramírez bolting.

I cursed. The bastard was making for our boat and, if he reached the *Santa Teresa*, he would be away with the Molucca Star. I had to stop him. I gave the signal to Walters and ran, aware of the eyes of my men on me, no doubt cursing their captain for a damn coward. There was nothing for it. I had to stop Ramírez or we would lose our fortunes.

With my crew's fusillade ringing in my ears, I slid down the cliffs, catching at palms and ferns, spraying sand as I hurried. I could see Ramírez below me, stumbling his way down to the beach. Out on the water, I saw two longboats putting out from the *Santa Teresa*, a couple of men in each, clearly coming to pick up their comrades. These were the boats that had intended to bring me as a prisoner to the *Santa Teresa* along with the Spaniards Ramírez had hidden in the ruins ahead of our arrival. As it was, only their captain was returning to them.

Dawn was breaking through heavy clouds and spots of rain had begun to fall. Ramírez had reached the sand now and was pelting towards the surf. I leaped the last few feet and landed heavily, rolling to absorb the shock. As soon as I was able, I was up and running, desperately trying to close the distance between myself and my quarry.

I was the leaner and faster of the two of us and, as I gained on him, I hurled myself forward, knocking

Ramírez to the sand. Coughing and spluttering, we both rolled and came up, drawing our cutlasses.

"Come with me, Rake!" Ramírez said. "It is the only way you can leave this place alive!"

"You've lost, Ramírez," I replied. "Half your men are slaughtered and I won't let you reach your ship alive."

"You are a fool! Even if you cut me down, that diamond you value so much is still aboard my ship! You cannot possibly get it, even if the savages spare some of your men."

He was right, of course. Killing him wouldn't get me the Molucca Star back but letting him go would see it vanish over the horizon before I could even get the *Azrael* underway.

I lunged at him with my cutlass, surprising him with my speed and force. He brought his own blade up to parry and steel rang against steel.

Pushing me to one side, he cut in at me and I thanked God that I had kept up my sword practice for he was a formidable opponent. I parried and fought back, our blades slithering and rasping like live serpents.

The rain was heavy now and our boots kicked up wet sand as I pressed on at Ramírez, pushing him towards the surf. I would drown the bugger if I had to, but I didn't have much time. The men in the boats had spotted us and were rowing towards us with all their might to aid their captain. Once they reached the shore, I would be as good as pork.

Ramírez swiped at my head and I ducked, narrowly losing my scalp. I thrust the tip of my blade into his abdomen and he cried out as the steel sank noiselessly into flesh.

Ripping the blade free I swung a downwards chop at the point where his neck met his shoulder but found myself blocked. The bastard still put up a good fight, even with a hole in his gut.

The approaching Spaniards had seen that their captain was badly injured and began firing on me with muskets. I was too far out of range and the sea too choppy for them to do much good.

The surf lapping around our ankles and the rain pelting us, we stood and stared at each other, both of us slick with water and Ramírez leaking blood. He was as a wounded lion and I knew that his desperation made him doubly dangerous.

He stabbed at me and I batted his blade aside. It was a weak thrust. He didn't have much strength left and he knew it. A second round of shots was fired from the boats, crackling through the rain like rolling thunder, closer now and I ducked, conscious of musket balls hitting the surf and sand near to our position.

Ramírez took my flinch as his chance and he lunged forward once more, putting all his weight behind his thrust. I was ready for him, blurry through he was through the rain that sheeted my eyes. I placed one foot behind me to spread my weight and held my blade out.

Ramírez fell onto its tip, his own blade catching me on the cheek as it passed by my head. I grunted as its keen edge opened up an ugly gash across my cheekbone but I held firm as Ramírez slid down the length of my blade, nearly to the hilt.

I turned sideways and flipped Ramírez into the surf, thrusting my boot down on his chest as I jerked my cutlass free. I held him down, pressing with all my weight as the surf rolled over him and back, pinkish with his blood. He choked and gurgled and then lay still.

I stepped off him and he bobbed up, his eyes still open and the two wounds I had given him leaking bloody streaks into the dark water. He was dead.

There were cries and curses in Spanish as the boats drew closer. More muskets fired and I flung myself flat in the water next to Ramírez's corpse. I was in a tight spot now.

I looked up and saw that the two boats had come about and were rowing back to the *Santa Teresa*. Their captain dead, they no doubt wished to be on their way although I would have thought that they might have taken their revenge on me.

Then, I saw my own crewmen stumbling down the cliffs towards me. Walters led them and they were soon running across the beach to my rescue.

"Ramírez?" Walters asked me, heaving for breath.

"Over there," I said, pointing to his body rolling in the surf. "I settled him for good but the Molucca Star is still aboard his ship. We must get to the *Azrael*. How many men did we lose?"

"None, by the grace of God," Walters replied. "The savages slaughtered the Spaniards and we gave them a volley as we made our escape. It doesn't look like they followed us."

We both glanced at the clifftops that were stark and bare against the leaden sky.

"Maybe enough blood was spilled to slake their thirst," I said. "We have been driven from their ruined city and I for one have no desire to set foot in it again."

"I agree with you there, Captain. But I wouldn't put it past those fellows to come back with an even larger force to push us into the sea."

"We must be long gone by then. Come! To the boat! The Spaniards are undermanned and have lost their captain. We might have a chance of taking the *Santa Teresa* if we act fast."

"Captain, she's putting out!" Rogers cried.

We all turned and looked as the *Santa Teresa*, her longboats hoisted, began to unfurl sail. The anchor was up and she drifted on the tide.

"Christ help us!" I said. "To the boat!"

By the time we were onboard, the *Santa Teresa* was making good headway into the distance. I ignored the blood streaming from my cut face as well as our surgeon's pleas and ordered the ship underway. It was only as the anchor was being drawn in that I allowed the surgeon to stitch me up.

We set sail as the day warmed and the clouds parted to reveal rays of sunlight. The *Santa Teresa* was a distant speck and I demanded all canvas crowded on to keep pursuit. Pitched to larboard, the *Azrael* cut through the waves, our repairs holding up well and proving that my men had done her proud.

"The crew are grumbling," Walters said to me as I stood aft, watching the bellying sails.

"I would have thought they would be happy to see the Yucatán coast vanishing behind us," I said.

"Oh, they are, Captain. No doubt about that. But it's the diamond, you see. Word has got around about the Spaniards pinching some great treasure from us along with the queen's heart. There is talk of you keeping loot for yourself."

I frowned in frustration. I had hoped that I might be able to get the diamond back in our possession before such talk began to undo me. But I suppose I owed the men some sort of explanation to quell rumours at the very least.

"Assemble the hands midships," I said to Walters. "I will address them and put this to rights."

Walters nodded and did as I asked. I retired to my cabin and stripped off my sodden and blood-stained clothes, putting on a fresh calico shirt and a black greatcoat. I brushed my hair and tied it back with a clean ribbon before stepping out on deck to speak to my men.

I could see from the sea of faces before me that I was not currently popular. Knitted brows and surly faces gazed up at me.

"Men!" I called down to them. "It has come to my attention that some ugly rumours are circulating about me. Some say that I kept a portion of loot for myself instead of sharing it with you as per the articles. There has been talk of a diamond, a large diamond that I did not declare to you out of pure greed. I do not seek to call out the spreaders of such lies but instead, I would like to take this opportunity to come clean and hopefully win your trust back. The truth is that this diamond does exist."

This caused much muttering between decks. My honesty had excited them.

"The diamond is called the Molucca Star," I continued. "Cut from some mine in the Dutch East Indies and hidden in Madagascar by Henry Avery and his men for twenty years. It is the size of a pebble and worth enough to make us all rich men forever."

The excitement bubbled up, many voices exultant but I could still hear the distrust.

"Did I keep this treasure of all treasures from you and pretend that it did not exist? Yes. I confess. I did keep it from you. But were my intentions to keep it for myself? No! Absolutely not! You must understand that a treasure of this size is a difficult thing to sell on in exchange for hard currency which we might all share. And, as I am sure you will all agree, that the fewer people who know about such a treasure the better. So, you see, I safeguarded the diamond for you, for us, until a suitable avenue of sale presents itself."

"But now you have lost it!" Fiaschetti cried. "Before we even knew that we were rich men, we have lost our fortunes!"

"Aye!" the crew angrily responded.

"Yes!" I cried back. "I share your anger! Captain Ramírez stole this treasure from us and even my killing him did not get it back! As we speak, our shared fortune is sailing to Havana. If the *Santa Teresa* reaches her destination, we will lose that diamond forever! That is why I am telling you this now. We must keep up the chase and sail like the devil himself in order to catch those Spaniards and reclaim our fortunes!"

The crew cried out their assent. I had them now. I had deflected their anger at me to the Spaniards who were sailing off with our treasure. We had a shared goal once more. Now we just had to reach out and claim it. The *Santa Teresa* was out of sight now, but we beat a course up the Straits of Yucatán, hoping to intercept her before she rounded the western tip of Cuba.

The following day, we passed Cuba's westernmost point and spotted our quarry adrift, its sails luffing.

"What are they playing at?" Walters said, squinting down his spyglass. "They're just sitting there."

"Could be a trap, Captain," said Rogers. "Should I run out the guns?"

"Yes," I said. "Beat to quarters. There's something not natural about them waiting for us so close to their destination. Await my order to fire and make damn sure we don't hole her below the waterline."

"I think she's been given a going over already," said Walters. "I see signs of battle damage."

"What!" I cried, seizing the glass from him. I looked down it and could see shattered gunwales and ragged sails caught in tangles of rigging. The *Santa Teresa* hadn't looked too pretty when she had set out, patched and fitted out with fresh timber, but now there were the unmistakable signs of battle damage.

"I'm thinking somebody's beaten us to it, Captain," said Walters.

My knuckles white as I gripped the spyglass, I ordered us to come alongside. As we drifted closer, what we saw made me sick to my gut and it wasn't the sight of blood, for I had become accustomed to that by now.

Somebody had ravaged the *Santa Teresa*, boarded her and butchered her crew. It looked like no quarter had been given. Bodies rolled between the guns, weapons still gripped in stiffened hands. We boarded her, weapons at the ready, still wary of ambush.

"Looks like our Spanish friends fought to the death," Walters said as we stepped our way around the bodies, grimacing at the blood that washed over our boots like bilge water.

"Knowing what they carried," I said, "wouldn't you? Wouldn't we all?"

We cautiously checked the Great Cabin and below for any sign of life. There was none.

"Rip this ship apart!" I said. "Search every inch for our lockbox."

We searched the ship from top to bottom, flung open every locker and rifled every cubbyhole. The lockbox was gone. I could have screamed at the blue sky, screamed at God for constantly cheating and toying with me.

"A sail!" Rogers cried from the quarterdeck.

"Spanish?" I called back. If friends of the late Captain Ramírez were to come upon us now, with the ship ransacked, her crew slaughtered and her captain gone, it would take some explaining to keep our heads on our shoulders.

"A sloop," Rogers said. "She flies the black!"

"A fellow pirate," I said to Walters. "Do you suppose they recognise the *Azrael*?"

"Perhaps," he replied. "Else they think to board us and the *Santa Teresa*."

I ordered everybody back aboard the *Azrael* and for the stricken *Santa Teresa* to be cut adrift. The unknown sloop approached us with the characteristic speed of a ship of that class and somebody hailed us.

"Captain Rake!" the voice shouted, showing that they knew the *Azrael*.

"It's Josiah Burgess!" said Walters. "One of Hornigold's men!"

We sighed with relief as the 10-gun sloop hove to alongside us and we invited Captain Burgess aboard.

"Well met, Rake," Burgess said. "We had thought you sunk in the hurricane for nobody has seen you for the best part of six months."

"We damn near were," I said. "We were wrecked on the coast of Yucatán. It's taken us this long to salvage our ship and put out to sea again."

"Aye, you look a little the worse for wear," Burgess said as he looked from me to my crew and then at the state of the *Azrael*. His eyes glanced over at the *Santa Teresa*. "What goes on here?"

"We've been chasing this Spaniard for a day and a half but somebody got to it before us. Have you seen any ships in the area?"

"The only one who passed us was Jennings in the *Bersheba* not a day ago."

"Who's that?"

"Henry Jennings is an old privateer based in Jamaica," Burgess said. "His ship the *Bersheba* is just about the finest Bermudan sloop I've ever set eyes on."

"A privateer wouldn't attack a Spanish ship," I said. "Unless Britain has declared war on Spain again during these months we have been beyond civilisation."

"Oh, you are a little naïve, Rake," Burgess said with a grin. "Privateers have always found it hard to remember that peace has been declared. Besides, Jennings is hardly one to let a little thing like the Treaty of Utrecht stand in the way of profit. And now, with the Spanish wrecks on the Florida coast tempting every man with a boat to go a-wrecking, Jennings will be waging his own private war against the Spanish to get his hands on as much loot as he can carry."

"What?" I exclaimed, barely comprehending him.

"You haven't heard?" Burgess said, his eyes wide. "You really have been out of the loop, haven't you?"

"What's this about Spanish wrecks?" Walters asked.

"The Spanish treasure fleet Hornigold has been so eagerly anticipating set out from Havana in July," Burgess replied. "We hadn't a chance of snatching anything from it, not against that firepower, but God in his mercy delivered the whole lot to us by hurling them against the Florida shore. The very hurricane that sent you to Yucatán sank His Catholic Majesty's fleet in shallow waters! The very sea bottom is littered with gold and silver, just there for the taking!"

I and every member of my crew goggled at him, scarcely able to believe what a stroke of fortune this was.

"Every man in Nassau has gone looking for the wrecks," Burgess continued. "And, with Jennings prowling these waters, it looks like Jamaica's privateers are in on the game too!"

"Christ almighty," said Walters. "When those wrecks are found, it'll be like flies to a honeypot!"

"And you can bet the Spaniards will be trying to salvage what they can," said Burgess. "It could get ugly. We're for the Florida coast to get in on the action while there is some left. What say you and I sail together, Rake?"

"Aye," I said, absent-mindedly. "We'll follow you to Florida. If what you say is true, then a fellow might get rich for very little effort."

Burgess returned to his own ship, eager to be sailing north-east. My crew were vocal about their enthusiasm as we got underway and followed in his wake, so much so that they had all but forgotten the diamond we were supposed to be chasing. The lure of Spanish gold in shallow waters, unprotected and in vast quantities was a potent force.

But my mind was on this Henry Jennings fellow and what he had snatched from me not a day since. I retired to my cabin and sat at my table, deep in thought. I was still mulling things over when Walters came in.

"Everything all right, Captain?"

"Aye, Walters. Just considering the paths ahead of us."

"It's the diamond, isn't it?"

"Yes. We were so close, Walters! I could practically smell it! And to lose it to a damnable spot of bad luck is almost more than I can bear."

"Lady Luck gives and takes in equal measure," Walters said. "I've seen enough of the world to reach that conclusion. We might have lost the diamond, but we are poised to enrich ourselves beyond measure at Spain's expense."

"We haven't necessarily lost the Molucca Star," I said, pensively.

"Jennings."

"Aye."

"He's a formidable opponent if crossed by all accounts."

"So am I."

Walters said nothing for a time and we sat in silence, listening to the shouting of the men on deck, the creaking of the timbers and the lapping water against the hull.

"Take care, Captain," he said at length.

"What do you mean?"

"That diamond has a peculiar hold over men. I've seen it before."

"Avery?"

"Aye. He couldn't abide losing it and spent the rest of his life trying to reclaim it. It killed him in the end; I've no doubt of it."

"I thought he died in poverty after being swindled by some alehouse rogues."

"That's what I mean. He was trying to scrape together funds for an expedition to Madagascar. To get back that diamond. It frightens me the lengths some men will go to for a bit of rock. Now, I'm not telling you what to do, Captain. All I'm saying is that a man who is content with an easier score – say, Spanish gold fished from the Florida Straits – would not be considered a fool. Not in my book at least."

"Thank you, Walters, I shall bear your philosophy in mind."

"Well," Walters cleared his throat. "I'd best be back on deck, making sure we are keeping pace with Burgess. It won't be long before we round the tip of Florida."

He left and I remained a while, considering his words. It shouldn't have surprised me that he was content to let the diamond go when other riches were close at hand. After all, he had his heart set on returning to England with wealth enough to ease the poverty of his family. But somehow, I *was* surprised. He had been part of the crew who had first stolen the Molucca Star. He had been a young man then and had spent most of his life either in possession of the stone or in pursuit of it. I wondered that he could so freely let it sail over the horizon. Perhaps I too should be content to do so.

But I wasn't.

Walters had a point, of course. He thought to warn me of Avery's fate. Perhaps the diamond did have an unnatural hold over men's hearts. A wise man might listen to his aging quartermaster. But perhaps I wasn't very wise, or at least had more courage than wisdom. I've been accused of such a thing before.

And neither was I a washed-out old salt like Avery trying to recapture the glory of his youth. Not yet at least. I was still young, still in my prime and I knew that I could make that diamond mine again.

And, as we rounded the tip of Florida, I swore to myself that I would.

Captain Philip Rake's adventures continue in 'Man of Fortune: The Further Adventures of Philip Rake'.

Printed in Great Britain
by Amazon

43819403R00138